STORMY
MISTY'S FOAL

THE MARGUERITE HENRY · ROUNDUP LIBRARY

STORMY
MISTY'S FOAL

By MARGUERITE HENRY

Illustrated by Wesley Dennis

RAND McNALLY & COMPANY
CHICAGO · NEW YORK · SAN FRANCISCO

Library of Congress Catalog Card Number: 63-13334

First paperback printing, 1970

Second paperback printing, 1971

Third paperback printing, 1972

Fourth paperback printing, 1973

Fifth paperback printing, 1974

Sixth paperback printing, 1975

Seventh paperback printing, 1975

Eighth paperback printing, 1976

Ninth paperback printing, 1977

Tenth paperback printing, 1978

Eleventh paperback printing, 1978

Twelfth paperback printing, 1979

Thirteenth paperback printing, 1980

DEDICATION

Dedicated to the boys and girls everywhere
whose pennies, dimes, and dollars helped restore
the wild herds on Assateague Island,
and who by their spontaneous outpouring of love
gave courage to the stricken people
of Chincoteague.

CONTENTS

Prologue

LAND ACROSS THE WATER

In the gigantic Atlantic Ocean just off the coast of Virginia a sliver of land lies exposed to the smile of the sun and the fury of wind and tide. It almost missed being an island, for it is only inches above the sea. The early Indians who poled over from the mainland to hunt deer and otter and beaver named this wind-rumpled island *Chin-co-teague,* "the land across the water."

Today a causeway, five miles long, connects it with the eastern shore of Virginia. Sometimes, when the sea breaks loose, it swallows the causeway. Then the people on the island are wholly isolated.

But most of the time Chincoteague enjoys the protection of a neighbor island, a great long rib of white sandy hills. The Indians called it *Assa-teague,* or "outrider." They named it well, for it acts as a big brother to Chincoteague, protecting it from crashing winds and the high waves of the Atlantic.

For many years now Assateague has been preserved as a wildlife refuge for ponies and deer and migrating waterfowl. On clear days herds of the wild ponies can be seen thundering along its shores, manes and tails flying in the wind.

Assateague, then, belongs to the wild things. But Chincoteague belongs to the people—sturdy island folk who live by raising chickens and by gathering the famous Chincoteague oysters and clams and diamond-backed terrapin. The one big joyous celebration of their year comes toward the end of July on Pony Penning Day. Then the volunteer firemen round up the wild ponies on Assateague, force them to swim the channel to Chincoteague, and pen them up for tourists and pony buyers who come from far and near. Of course, only the young colts are gentle enough to be sold. The money from the auction is used to buy fire-fighting equipment to protect the fisherfolk and chicken farmers who live on Chincoteague.

There is one family whom the firemen look upon as friendly competitors in their yearly pony sale. They are the Beebes—Grandpa and Grandma and their grandchildren, Paul and Maureen. Except for Grandma, whose father was a sea captain, they call themselves "hossmen." They are in the pony business the year around. Their place at the southern end of the island is known simply as Pony Ranch.

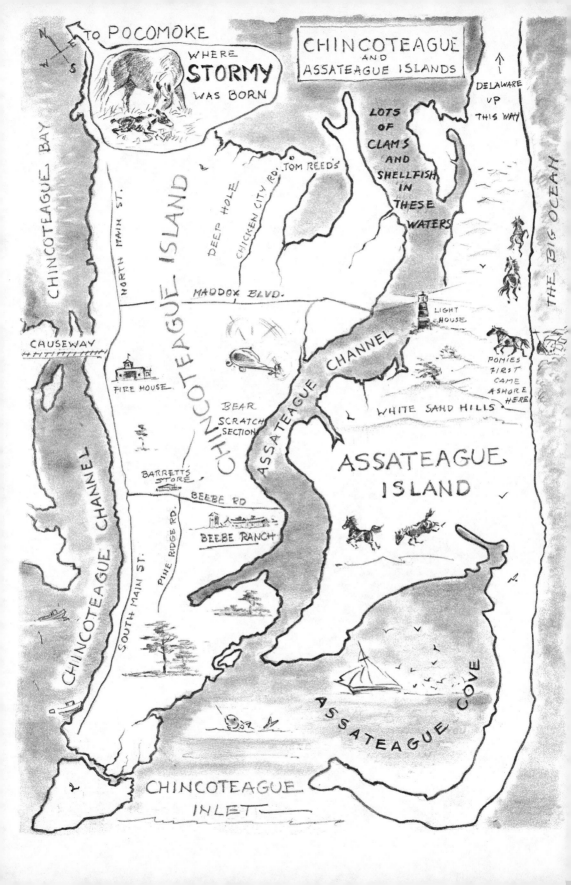

STORMY
MISTY'S FOAL

Chapter 1

BEFORE THE STORM

THE CLOCK on the shelf pointed to five as young Paul Beebe, his hair tousled and his eyes still full of sleep, came into the kitchen. Paul did not even glance at the clock, though it was a handsome piece, showing the bridge of a ship with a captain at the wheel. For Paul, his banty rooster was clock enough.

Grandpa Beebe was bent over the sink, noisily washing his face. He came up for air, his head cocked like a robin listening for worms.

"Just hark at that head rooster!" he grinned, his face dripping. He reached for the towel Grandma was handing him. "That banty," he went on as he mopped his face, "is

17

better than any li'l ole tinkly alarm clock. Why, he's even
more to depend on than that fancy ticker yer sea-farin'
father brung us from France." He gave Grandma a playful
wink. "What's more, ye never have to wind him up, and I
never knowed him to sleep overtime."

"Me neither," Paul said, "even when it's cloudy."

The old man and the boy went thudding in their sock
feet to the back hall, to their jackets hanging over the wash
tubs and their boots standing side by side.

Grandma's voice tailed them. "Wrap up good now.
Wind's bitter." She came to the doorway and looked sharply
at Paul. "I got to brew some sassafras roots to perten ye up.

I declare, ye look older and tireder than yer grandpa."

"Who wouldn't look tuckered out?" Grandpa asked in pride. "Paul took the midnight watch on Misty."

"This household," Grandma sputtered, "does more worritin' over Misty having a colt than if she was a queen birthin' a crown prince."

"Well, she is!" Paul exclaimed. "She's a movie queen."

"Yup," Grandpa joined in. "Name me another Chincoteague pony who's a star of a movin' picture like Misty is. And her being famous—well, it's made a heap o' difference to Pony Ranch."

Paul nodded vehemently. "Yes, Grandma. You know we sell more ponies because of her, and we can buy better fodder, and this summer I'm going to build her a fine stable and . . ."

"And I'll never hear the end of it!" Grandma grumbled. "Our place is a reg'lar mecca for folks comin' to see her, and when she has her colt—land o' mercy!—they'll be thicker'n oysters in a pie."

Paul and Grandpa were out the door. Grandma's sputtering bothered them no more than a mosquito before the fuzz comes off its stinger.

A faint light had begun to melt the darkness and there was a brim of dawn on the sea. The wind, blowing from the southwest in strong and frequent gusts, rippled the old dead marsh grasses until they and the waves were one.

As Grandpa and Paul hurried to the barn, a golden-furred collie leaped down from his bed in the pickup truck and came galloping to meet them.

"Hi, Skipper!" Paul gave him a rough-and-tumble greet-

19

ing, but his heart wasn't in it. He caught at his grandfather's sleeve. "Grandpa!" he said, talking fast. "Buck Jackson's got some she-goats up to his place."

"So?"

"Well, if Misty should be bad off . . ."

"What in tarnation you gettin' at?"

"Maybe we'd ought to buy a goat, just in case . . ."

"In case *what*?"

"Misty couldn't give enough milk for her colt."

The old man pulled himself loose from Paul. "Get outen my way, boy. What's the sense to begin worryin' now? We got chores to do. Listen at them ponies raisin' a ruckus to be fed, and all the ducks and geese a-quackin' and a-clackin' and carryin' on. Everybody's hungry, includin' me."

"But, Grandpa!" Paul was insistent. "You yourself said April or May colts have a better chance of living than March ones."

The old man stopped in mid-stride. "It just ain't fittin' fer colts to drink goat's milk," he said gruffly. "'Specially Misty's colt." He clumped off toward the corncrib, muttering and shaking his head.

Paul skinned between the fence rails and ran toward the made-over chicken coop that was Misty's barn. He heard her whinnying in a low, rumbly tone. His heart pumping in expectancy, he unbolted her door. She came to him at once, touching nostrils as if he were another pony, then nibbling his straw-colored hair so that he couldn't see what he was looking for. Gently he pushed her away and stepped back. He looked underneath and around her. But there was no little colt lying in the straw. He looked at her sides. They were heavily

20

rounded, just as they had been at midnight, and the night before, and the night before that.

"Surely it'll come today," Paul said to her, trying to hide his disappointment. "For a while it can live right in here with you. But soon as school's out, I got to build us more stalls. Maureen can help."

"Help what?" came a girl's voice.

Paul turned to see his sister standing on tiptoe looking over his shoulder. "Help me pump," he added hastily.

"Paul! Maureen!" Grandpa shouted from the corncrib. "Quit lallygaggin'! Water them ponies afore they die o' thirst."

Most of Grandpa's herd were still away on winter pasture at Deep Hole on the north end of the island. There the pine trees grew in groves and the whole area was thickly underbrushed so the ponies could keep warm, out of the wind. And they could fend for themselves, living on wild kinksbush and cord grass.

But here at Pony Ranch Grandpa kept only his personal riding horses—Billy Blaze, and dependable old Watch Eyes— as well as a few half-wild ponies from Assateague. All winter long this little bunch of ragged creatures ran free out on the marshland, fenced in only by the sea. But every morning they came thundering in, manes and tails blowing like licks of flame. At the gate they neighed shrilly, demanding fresh water and an ear or two of corn. It was Paul's and Maureen's duty to pump gallons and gallons of water into an old tin wash tub and dole out the ears of corn.

"It's your turn to pump," Maureen said. "I'll let the bunch in, and I'll parcel out the corn."

"Don't you start bossing me!" Paul retorted. "One grandma to a house is enough." Then he grinned in superiority. "You pump too slow, anyway. Besides, it develops my muscles for roundup time."

As Maureen let the ponies into the corral, two at a time, they dashed to the watering tub and drank greedily. Paul could hardly pump fast enough. He drew in a breath. Cold or no, this was the best time of day. And no matter how hard and fast his arms worked, nor how many times he had to fill the tub, he liked doing it. It made him feel big and strong, almost godlike, as if he had been placed over this hungry herd and was their good provider. He liked the sounds of their snorting and fighting to be first, and he liked to watch them plunge their muzzles deep in the water and suck it in between their teeth. He even liked it when they came up slobbering and the wind sent spatters against his face.

Usually Misty was first at the watering tub, for she ran free with the others out on the marsh. But now that her colt was due she was kept in her stall, where she could be watched constantly. So Paul watered her last. He wanted her to take her time and to drink her fill without a bunch of ponies squealing and pawing at the gate, getting her excited. But today, even with the tub all to herself, she acted skittery as dandelion fluff—not drinking, but playing with the water, blowing at it until it made ripples.

Paul grew alarmed. Why wasn't she drinking? Did that mean it would be soon? Or was she sick inside? He stopped pumping and gave himself up to bittersweet worry. It could be this very morning, and then he'd have to stay home from school to help dry off the colt and to see that Misty was a good nurser.

"Paul! Maureen!" Grandpa's voice boomed like a foghorn. "Put Misty in and come help me feed." He stood there in the barnyard with his head thrown back, shrilling to the heavens: *"Wee-dee-dee-dee! Wee-dee-dee-dee!"*

The call was a magnet, pulling in the fowl—wild ones from the sky, tame ones from the pasture. Geese and ducks and gulls, cocks and chickens and guinea hens came squawking. Above the racket Grandpa barked out his orders. "You children shuck off this corn for the critters." He handed them a coal scuttle heaped high with ears. "I got to police the migrators. Dad-blasted if I'll let them Canadian honkers hog all the feed whilst my own go hungry."

Faster than crows the children shelled out the corn until the scuttle held nothing but cobs, and at last the barnyard settled down to a picking and a pecking peace.

Grandpa scanned the sky for stragglers, but he saw none. Only gray wool clouds, and an angry wind pulling them apart. "Looks like a storm brewing, don't it?"

Paul laughed. "You should've been a weatherman, Grandpa, 'stead of a hossman. You're always predicting."

"Allus right, ain't I? Here, Maureen, you run and hang up the scuttle. I can whiff Grandma's bacon clean out here, and I'm hungry enough to eat the haunches off'n a grasshopper."

It was a bumper breakfast. The table was heaped with stacks of hotcakes and thick slices of bacon. Grandpa took one admiring look at his plate before he tackled it. "Nobody," he said, "not nobody but yer Grandma understands slab bacon. Over to the diner in Temperanceville they frazzle all the sweetness outen it so's there ain't no fat left. Tastes like my old gumboots."

Grandma beamed. If someone had given her a string of diamonds or a bunch of florist flowers, she couldn't have looked more pleased. "Clarence," she asked in her best company voice, "will you have honey or molasses on your hotcakes?"

"How kin I have *mo'* 'lasses when I ain't had *no* 'lasses at all?"

Paul and Maureen giggled at Grandpa's old joke—not just to please him but because it tickled them, and when they went visiting they sprang it on their cousins every chance they got.

Quiet settled down over the table except for the clatter of forks and Grandpa slurping his coffee. With second helpings talk began.

"Grandma," Paul asked, "how'd you like a few goats? A billy maybe, but a she-goat for sure? Y'see, she could be a nurser just in case."

Grandma put down her fork. "Paul Beebe! I swan, it must be mental telegraphy. Why, only last night I dreamt we had a hull flock of goats, and Misty friended with a nice old nanny and she let her kid run with Misty's baby and they'd butt each other and play real cute."

Grandpa clamped his hands over both ears. "I'm deef!"

25

he bellowed. "I heerd nary a word!" He got up from the table. "Six o'clock!" he announced. "You children light out and clean Misty's stall. Schooltime'll be here afore ye know it. The sea's in a fret today and there's a look to the sky I don't like. No time for gabbin'."

"Pshaw," Grandma said. "My daddy, who was captain of the . . ."

"Yes, Idy," he mimicked, "yer daddy, who was captain of the *Alberta,* the last sailing vessel here to Chincoteague, he'd say—wa-ll, *what'd* he say?"

"He'd say," Grandma repeated, proud of her knowledge of the sea, " 'There's barely a riffle of waves in the bay. Glass is down low, and we're due for a change in the weather.' But, Clarence, aren't we always in for a change?"

Chapter 2

A DUCK IN THE HORSE TROUGH

WHEN MISTY's stall was mucked out and her manger filled with sweet hay, Paul and Maureen burst into the kitchen, laughing and out of breath.

"*You* say it, Maureen."

"No, you."

Paul shuffled his feet. He glanced sidelong at Grandma. "Me and Maureen . . . I and Maureen . . . Maureen and I . . . Well," he blurted, "we'd like to say some Bible verses, with a little change to one of them."

Grandma almost dropped the cup she was wiping. She spun around, smiling in surprise. "There's no call to blush about quoting from the Good Book," she said. "It's a fine thing."

Paul swallowed hard. His eyes flew to Maureen's. "You say it," he urged.

Maureen looked straight at Grandma. "Last Sunday in church," she spoke quickly and earnestly, "Preacher read: 'There's a time to sow and a time to reap.' "

"Yes, that's what he said," Paul nodded. "And he said, 'There's a time to cry and a time to laugh.' "

" 'And a time to love and a time to hate,' " Maureen added.

Paul began shouting like the preacher. " 'There's a time to make war and a time to make peace.' "

"How 'bout that!" Grandma's eyes were shinier than her spectacles. "You heard every bit of the message, and here I thought you two was doing crossword puzzles all the time! Now then, what's the made-up part?" she asked encouragingly.

The answer came loud and in unison: "There's a time to go to school and a time to stay home."

"And just when is that?" Grandma demanded.

"When a mare is ready to foal," Paul said with a look of triumph.

The kitchen grew very still. Grandma shook out the damp towel and hung it above the stove. To gain thinking time she put the knives and forks in the drawer and each teaspoon in the spoon rack. Then she glanced from one eager face to the other. "You two ever see a wild mare birthing her young'un?"

They both shook their heads.

"Nor have I. Nor yer Grandpa neither." She looked far out on the marsh, at the ponies grazing peacefully. "Well, the way the mares do it," she said at last, "is to go off a day, mebbe more, and hide in some lonely spot. And the next time you see her come to the watering trough, there's a frisky youngster dancing alongside. Why, one mare swum clean across the channel to Hummocky Isle to have her baby, and three days later they both come back and joined the herd— even that little baby swum."

"But *they're* wild, Grandma," Paul said. "Misty's different. She's lived with people since she was a tiny foal."

Grandma took an old cork and a can of powder and began scouring the stains on her carving knives. She nodded slowly."And Misty's smart. If she needs help, she'll come up here to the fence and let us know right smart quick, same's she does when she's thirsty. Now you both wash up and change yer clothes. You touched off the wrong fuse when you quoted Bible verses to get excused from school."

"But, Grandma," Paul persisted, "how can Misty tell anyone she needs help when Grandpa's in town shucking oysters, and we're trapped in school and . . ."

Grandma didn't answer; yet somehow she interrupted. She handed Maureen a pitcher of milk and a saucedish. As if by magic Wait-a-Minute, a big tiger-striped cat, appeared from under the stove and began lapping the milk even before Maureen finished pouring it.

"Tell you what," Grandma said after a moment's thought. "I promise to go out every hour and look in on Misty."

"You will?"

"That I will."

"And will you telephone school in case she needs us?"

"I'll even promise you that. Cross my heart!"

Somewhat appeased, Paul and Maureen washed and hurried into their school clothes. When they dashed out of the house, Grandpa was climbing into his truck. "Hop in," he said. "I'll give ye a lift." He put the key in the ignition, but he didn't start the car. A blast of surprise escaped him. "Great balls o' fire! Look!"

"What is it, Grandpa?"

He pointed a finger at a big white goose up-ended in the watering tub. "Jes' look at him waller! Now," he said in awe, "I got a sure omen."

"Of what?" both children asked.

Grandpa recited in a whisper:

> "A goose washin' in the horse trough
> Means tomorrow we'll be bad off."

"Who says so?" Paul wanted to know.

"My Uncle Zadkiel was a weather predictor, and he said geese in the trough is a fore-doomer of storm."

Grandpa started the car, a troubled look on his face.

The day at school seemed never-ending. Maureen answered questions like a robot. She heard her own voice say, "Christopher Columbus was one of the first men who believed the world was round. So he went east by sailing west."

"Very good, Maureen. You may sit down."

But Maureen remained standing, staring fixedly at the map over the blackboard. Her mind suddenly went racing across the world, and backward in time, to a tall-masted ship. Not the one that Columbus sailed, but the one that brought the ponies to Assateague. And she saw a great wind come up, and she watched it slap the ship onto a reef and crack it open like the shell of an egg, and she saw the ponies spewed into the sea, and she heard them thrashing and screaming in all that wreckage, and one looked just like Misty.

"*I said,*" the teacher's voice cut through the dream, "*you may sit down, Maureen.*"

The class tittered as she quickly plopped into her seat.

In Paul's room an oral examination was about to take place. "We'll begin alphabetically," Miss Ogle announced. "Question number one," she said in her crisp voice. "With all books closed, explain to the class which is older, the earth or the sea, and where the first forms of life appeared. We'll begin with Teddy Appleyard."

Teddy stood up, pointing to a blood-splotched handkerchief he held to his nose. He was promptly excused.

"Now then, Paul Beebe, you are next."

Dead silence.

"We'll begin," the teacher raised her voice, "with Paul Be-ee–be-ee," and she stretched out his name like a rubber band. But even then it didn't reach him.

He was not there in the little white schoolhouse at all. In his mind he was back at Pony Ranch and Misty had broken out of her stall and gone tearing down the marsh. And in his fantasy he saw the colt being born, and while it was all wet and new, it was sucked slowly, slowly down into the miry bog. There was no sound, no whimper at all. Just the wind squeaking through the grasses.

Tap! Tap! Miss Ogle rapped her pencil sharply on the desk. "Boys and girls," she said, "you have all heard of people suffering from nightmares. But I declare, Paul Beebe is having a *daymare*."

The class burst into noisy laughter, and only then did the mad dream break apart.

Back home in Misty's shed all was warm contentment. There was plenty of hay in the manger, good hay with here and there some sweet bush clover, and a block of salt hollowed out from many lickings so that her tongue just fitted. She worked at it now in slow delight, her tongue-strokes stopping occasionally as she turned to watch a little brown hen rounding out a nest in a corner of the stall. Fearlessly the hen let Misty walk around her as if she liked company, and every now and again she made soft clucking sounds.

Out on the marsh Billy Blaze and Watch Eyes, pretending to be stallions, fought and neighed over the little band of mares. Misty looked out at them for a long time, then went to her manger and slowly began munching her hay. The hen, now satisfied with her nest, fluffed out her feathers and settled herself to lay one tiny brown egg.

Contentment closed them in like a soft coccoon.

Chapter 3

A BODY WITH A PURPOSE

RIGHT AFTER school Paul and Maureen rushed into Misty's stall, almost in panic. Things should be happening, and they weren't. Grandpa Beebe joined them. "You two hold her head," he ordered. He put his stubbly cheek and his ear against Misty's belly.

"Feel anything? Hear anything?" Paul whispered.

"Not jes' now. Likely the little feller's asleep." He bent down and felt of Misty's teats. Gently he tried to milk them. "Some mares is ticklish," he explained, "and they kick at their colt when it tries to nurse. I aim to get her used to the idee."

"You getting any milk?" Maureen asked.

Grandpa shook his head. "Reckon Misty ain't quite ready to have her young'un. But no use to worry. Now then, I'd like for ye two to do me a favor."

"What is it, Grandpa?"

"I want ye to climb aboard Watch Eyes and Billy Blaze, 'cause today noon it 'peared to me Billy was going gimpy. You children try him out and see which leg's causin' the trouble."

Paul and Maureen were glad of something to do. The way Grandpa talked made them feel like expert horsemen. Quickly they bridled the ponies, swung up bareback, and took off. Paul stayed a few lengths behind on Watch Eyes, calling commands to Maureen on Billy Blaze.

"Walk him!"

Ears swinging, head nodding, Billy stepped out big and bold. Almost bouncy.

"Trot him!"

Again he went sound, square on all four corners.

"Whoa! Turn! Come this way."

Maureen pulled up, laughing. "Except for his being so shaggy," she said, "he could be a horse in a show, his gaits are so smooth. Grandpa knew it all the time."

"Of course. He just wanted us to stop fussing over Misty. I'll race you, Maureen."

It was fun racing bareback across the marsh. The rising wind excited the horses, made them go faster, as if they wanted to be part of it. And it was fun to round up the mares and drive them down the spit of land, stopping just short of the sea. It was even fun arguing.

"Maureen, you got to do the pumping tonight."

"I don't either. I got to gather the eggs."

"All right, Miss Smarty, then you can just mend that chicken fence, too."

It ended by both of them repairing the fence and both

taking turns pumping water. Afterward, they charged into the house, glowing and hungry.

Grandma promised an early supper of oyster pie. "And then," she said, "if you can trust me to keep watch on Misty, you can drive with yer Grandpa over to Deep Hole to the Reeds' house. Mrs. Reed's got a pattern I want to copy for our apron sale."

"*I'll* take ye up on yer offer, Idy," Grandpa agreed quickly. "It'll give me a chance to see how my herd's doin' up there on winter pasture."

But about that time odd things began to happen. A lone marsh hen came bustling across the open field toward the house. Paul saw her first. He was at the table in the sitting room, painting a duck decoy.

"Look! Come quick!" he shouted to the household. "A marsh hen's coming to pay us a call!"

Maureen hurried into the room to see. Grandpa and

Grandma almost collided, trying to get through the door at the same time.

"Jumpin' mullets!" Grandpa whistled. "In all my born days I never see a marsh hen walkin' on dry ground."

"Can't say I have either," Grandma agreed. "They're timid folk, ain't they?"

"Yup, only feel safe in a marsh, like a rabbit in a briar patch."

"I saw one, one day," Paul said, "walk right across the causeway."

"Pshaw!" Grandpa whittled him down to size. "*Every-one's* seen 'em do that. They're just makin' a quick trip acrost, from one marsh to another. But *this* little hen has made a journey. For her it's like travelin' to the moon."

Grandma nodded. "To my notion, she's a body with a purpose. She's tryin' to find a hidey-hole. Wonder what's frighted her?"

They all watched as the hen made her way to the high ground near the smokehouse and settled down on the doorstep as though she'd found a safe harbor.

Everybody went back to work except Grandpa. He crossed the room to the window that faced the channel. "Great guns!" he exclaimed. "Look at how our lone pine tree is bent! Why, the wind's switched clean around from sou'west to nor'east! And look at the sky—it's black as the inside of a cow." Suddenly he sucked in his breath. "The tide," he gasped, "it's almost up to our field!"

"Only nacherel," Grandma called from the kitchen. "We're in the time of the new moon, and a new moon allus means a fuller tide."

But Grandpa wasn't listening. He began pacing from one room to the other. "Any storm warnings on the radio today, Idy?" he asked.

"No," Grandma said thoughtfully, "except the Coast Guard gave out small-craft warnings this morning. But three outen five days in March, they hoist that red flag."

"Even so," Grandpa said, "me and Paul better light out and put the ponies in the hay house for safety."

Paul dropped his paintbrush and started for the door.

"Bring in more wood for the stove," Grandma called after them.

Darkness was coming on quickly and the wind had sharpened, bringing with it a fine whipping rain. The old

man and the boy whistled the ponies in from the marsh. They
came at a gallop, eager to get out of the weather. It wasn't
often they were given all the hay they could eat, and warm
shelter too.

Paul grabbed a bundle of hay and ran to Misty's stall.
He found her stomping uneasily and biting at herself, but he
blamed the little colt inside her, not the weather. The wind
fluttered the cobwebs over the window at the back of her stall.
He nailed a gunny sack to the frame to keep the cold out.
Then, feeling satisfied, he gave Misty a gentle pat on the
rump. As he went out, he bolted both the top and the bottom
of her door.

He joined Grandpa, who was gathering up four fluffy
black mallards, too young to fly, and putting them in a high
cage in the hay house. The peacocks and banties were already
roosting in the pine trees Wherever Paul and Grandpa went,

Skipper ran ahead, enjoying the wind and the feeling of danger and excitement. At the kitchen door he left them, jumping into his bed in the truck. Habit was stronger than the wind.

Inside the house, all was warmth and comfort—the fire crackling in the stove, the oyster pie sending forth rich fragrances, and from the radio in the sitting room a cowboy's voice was throbbing:

> "Oh, give me a home
> Where the buffalo roam,
> And the deer and the antelope . . ."

The word "play" never came. The music stopped as if someone had turned it off. At the same instant the kitchen went black as a foxhole.

A strange, cold terror entered the house. For a long moment everyone stood frozen. Then Grandma spoke in her gayest voice, which somehow didn't sound gay at all. "We'll just eat our supper by candlelight. It'll be like a party."

She found the flashlight on the shelf over the sink, and pointed its beam inside a catch-all drawer. "I got some candles in here somewheres," she said, poking in among old party favors and odds and ends of Christmas wrappings.

Grandpa struck a match and held it ready. "Yer Grandma looks like Skipper diggin' up an old bone. Dag-bite-it!" he exclaimed. "I'm burnin' my fingers." The match sputtered and died of itself.

"I'm 'shamed to say," Grandma finally admitted, "but I recomember now, I gave my old candles to the family that moved in on Gravel Basket Road. They hadn't any electric in the house. What's more, I loaned 'em our lantern."

Grandpa's voice was quick and stern. "Paul! You drive my pickup over to Barrett's Store and get us a gallon of coal oil. Maureen, you crunch up some newspaper to —"

"Clarence!" Grandma was shocked. "Paul's not old enough to drive, and hark to that wind."

"Idy, this here's an emergency. I'm the onliest one knows jes' where in the attic to put my hand on the old ship's lantern off'n the *Alberta*. Besides, Barrett's is jes' up Rattlesnake Ridge, as fer as a hen can spit."

Paul was out the door in a flash and Grandpa was pulling down the ladder in the hall to the crawl-space in the attic. As he climbed up he muttered loud enough for Grandma to hear, "Wimmenfolk and worry, cups and saucers, wimmenfolk and worry!"

When he came back with the lantern, he handed it to Maureen. "Like I said, honey, you crunch up some newspaper and give this chimney a good cleaning, and then pick the black stuff off'n the wick. Here, ye can use my flashbeam to work by."

Seconds passed, and the minutes wore slowly on. It was past time for Paul to be back. Grandpa peered out the window, trying to pull car lights out of the dark. He wished Grandma would not just sit there, hands folded in prayer. He wished she'd sputter and scold. He wished she'd say something. Anything.

He even wished Maureen would say something. But she was intent on her work. "That's good enough, honey. Better shut the flashbeam off now. We may be needing it for trips to the barn," he added seriously.

When at last Paul burst into the house, he set the can of coal oil on the table without a word. Grandma quickly opened it and poured some in the base of the lantern.

"Wa-al?" Grandpa asked as he struck a match and lighted the wick. He turned it slowly up and watched the flame steady. "Where ye been? Yer Grandma's nigh crazy with worry over ye. What took ye so long?"

"I drove around to see how bad the storm is."

"And how bad is it?"

"Bad. *Real* bad."

"What you lookin' so ashy about?"

"I got bogged down in the sand on Main Street. The bay water's coming right over the road and lots of cars are stuck. Fire Chief had to push me out."

"Oh . . ." Grandpa looked concerned. "Ye'd better run my truck up to that high place by the fence, Paul. If this wind keeps up, no tellin' how far she'll shove the tide."

Chapter 4

LET THE WIND SCREECH

THE STORM was sharpening as Paul moved the truck.
If he hurried, he could look in on Misty once more. Skipper
read his thoughts and leaped out with him, but he didn't dash
ahead. He hugged close to Paul, his action saying, "Two
creatures against the storm are better than one."

The wind swept down upon them and struck with an
iron-cold blast. It took Paul's breath. He had to fight his way,
reaching up, grasping for the clothesline. He might not be
able to get out again. Suppose Misty'd already had her colt
and was too frightened to take care of it? Suppose it suffocated
in its birthing bag because no one was there to tear it open?

He stumbled over a tree root, and only the clothesline
kept him from sprawling. But now he had to let go. He had
reached the post where the line turned back to the house. He

was almost to the corral. Now he was there. He squeezed through the bars. He reached the shed, crying out Misty's name.

She came to him, her breath warm on his face. He put both arms around her body. The colt was still safe inside her. A wave of love and relief washed over him as he leaned against her, enjoying the warmth of her body. He stood there, wondering what she would say to him if she could, wondering whether she was thinking at all, or just feeling content, rubbing up against a fellow-creature for comfort.

Skipper nosed in between them, nudging first one and then the other, wanting to be part of the kinship.

"You can stay in here tonight, feller," Paul said. "You'll keep each other warm." Reluctantly he left them and headed toward the house. The wind and rain were at his back now, pushing him along as if he were in the way.

The kitchen felt cozy and warm by contrast, and the acrid smell of the coal oil seemed pleasant. The light, though feeble, didn't hide the worry on Grandma's and Grandpa's faces. But Maureen was humming and happy, her head bent over small squares of paper. Wait-a-Minute was perched on her shoulder, purring noisily.

Paul picked up the cat, warming his fingers in her fur. "What you doing, Maureen?" he asked.

She folded one of the squares and held it up in triumph. "Isn't it exciting, Paul?"

"What's it supposed to be?"

"Why, a birth announcement, of course."

"Gee willikers! Horsemen don't send out announcements!"

"I know that. But Misty's different. Everybody's heard

how she came from the wild ones on Assateague and chose to live with us 'stead of her own kin."

Paul held the folder close to the light. He studied it curiously and in surprise. On the top sheet were three sketches of horses' heads. The one on the left was unmistakably Misty, and the one on the right could have been any horse-creature except that it was carefully labeled *"Wings."* Between the two, in a small oval, there was a whiskery colt's face and underneath it a dash where the name could be printed in later.

"Right purty, eh, Paul?" Grandpa asked.

"Look at the inside," Grandma urged.

?

MISTY
OF CHINCOTEAGUE

THE PHANTOM
OF ASSATEAGUE

THE PIED PIPER
OF ASSATEAQUE

WILD MARE - UNKNOWN

WINGS
OF CHINCOTEAGUE
(NEVER BEEN RIDDEN)

WILD STALLION - UNKNOWN

Paul opened it and read aloud: *"Little No-Name out of Misty by Wings. Misty out of The Phantom by The Pied Piper. Wings out of a wild mare by a wild stallion."* He pulled at his forelock, thinking and studying the pedigree.

"One thing wrong," he said with authority.

Maureen's lips quivered. "Oh, Paul, I can't help it if I can't draw good as you."

"It's not that, Maureen. The pictures are nice. Better than I could do," he admitted honestly. "But in pedigrees the stallion's name and *his* family always come first."

"But, Paul, remember how Misty's mother outsmarted the roundup men every Pony Penning until she birthed Misty? The Pied Piper was penned up every year, and if it hadn't been for Misty, likely The Phantom never, ever would of been captured. Remember?"

" 'Course I remember! I brought her in, didn't I?" He stopped and thought a moment. "But I reckon you're right, Maureen. This pedigree *is* different. Misty and The Phantom should come first."

"These children got real hoss sense, Idy," Grandpa bragged. "I'm so dang proud o' them I could go around with my chest stickin' out like a penguin." He strutted across the room, trying to stamp out his worry.

Suddenly the lights flashed on and a voice blared over the radio: ". . . is in the grip of the worst blizzard of the winter. Twelve inches of snow have fallen in central Virginia and still more to come. At Atlantic City battering seas have undercut the famous board walk. Great sections of it have collap . . ." The voice was cut off between syllables as if the announcer had been strangled. Again the house went dark,

47

except for the flame in the lantern and a rim of yellow around the stove lids.

"Supper's ready," Grandma sang out in forced cheerfulness. "Guess we can all find our mouths in the dark. These oysters," she said as she ladled the gravy over each plate, "is real plump, and the batter bread is light as a . . . as a . . ."

"As a moth?" Paul prompted.

"Well, mebbe not that light," Grandma replied.

They all sat down in silence, listening to the sound of the wind spiralling around the house. Suddenly Grandpa pushed his chair back. "I can't eat a thing, Idy," he said. "But you all eat. I just now thought 'bout something."

"'Bout what, Clarence?"

"'Bout Mr. Terry."

Grandma put down her fork. "That's the man who moved here to Chincoteague last fall, ain't it?"

As Grandpa nodded his head, Paul broke in. "He's the man who has to live in a kind of electric cradle."

"That's the one. His bed has to rock, Idy, or he dies. And now with the electric off, he may be gaspin' for air like a fish out o' water. Me and Paul could go over and pump that bed by hand."

He hurried into the sitting room, to the telephone on the little table by the window. "Lucy," he told the operator, "please to get me Miz' Terry. She could be needin' help."

Grandma put Grandpa's plate back on the stove. Everyone stopped eating to listen.

"That you, Miz' Terry?" Grandpa's voice boomed above wind and storm.

Pause.

"You don't know me, but this here's Clarence Beebe over to Pony Ranch, and I was jes' a-wonderin' how ye'd like four mighty strong arms to pump yer husband's bed by hand."

There was a long pause.

"Ye don't say! Wal now, ain't that jes' fine. But ye'll call me if ye need hand-help, eh?"

Grandpa strode back to the table, sat down and stuffed his napkin under his chin.

"What did Miz' Terry say?" asked Grandma, setting his plate in front of him.

Grandpa ate with gusto. He slurped one oyster, then another, before he would talk. "Why, ye'd never believe it, Idy, how quick people think! First, Charlie Saunders, who's in charge of the hull Public Service—he calls Miz' Terry and warns her 'bout the wind bein' high and the electric liable to go out, so she calls Henry Leonard down to the hardware store, and almost afore she hung up there was a boy knockin' at her door with a generator and some gasoline to run it."

Grandpa sighed in satisfaction. "So let the wind screech," he said, "and let the rain slap down, and let the tide rip. We're all here together under our snug little roof."

A good feeling came into the room. The lantern flame seemed suddenly to shine brighter and the homely kitchen with its red-checkered cloth became a thing of beauty.

Chapter 5

NINETY HEAD

B EFORE SECOND helpings the storm struck in full fury. It came whipping down the open sea like some angry, flailing giant. It shook the house, rattled the shutters, clawed at the shingles.

The kitchen, so snug and secure a moment ago, suddenly seemed fragile as an eggshell.

Grandpa and the children rushed to the sitting-room window. They could not see beyond the windowpane itself. Only wind-driven rain, streams of rain, slithering down the glass, bubbling at its edges. Every few moments one ghostly beam from the lighthouse over on Assateague sliced through the downpour—then all was blackness again.

Maureen tugged at Grandpa's sleeve. "Grandpa! What if Misty's baby is being born? Right now? Will it die?"

Paul, too, felt panic. "Grandpa!" he yelled. "Let's go out there."

But Grandpa stood mesmerized. He wasn't seeing this storm. He was in another storm long ago, and he was thinking: " 'Twas the wind and waves that wrecked the Spanish ship and brought the ponies here. What if the wind and waves should swaller 'em and take 'em back again!" In his darkened thoughts he could see the ponies fighting the wreckage, fighting for air, fighting to live.

And suddenly he began to pray for all the wild things out on a night like this. Then he thought to himself, "Sakes alive! I'm taking over Idy's work." He turned around and saw her at the sink washing the dishes as if storms were nothing to fret about. A flash of understanding shuttled between them. They would both hide their fears from the children.

Paul's voice was now at the breaking point. And Grandpa knew the questions without actually hearing the words. But he had no answer. He, too, was worried about Misty. He put one arm around Paul and another around Maureen, drawing them away from the window, pulling them down beside him on the lumpy couch.

"There, there, children, hold on," he soothed. "Buckle on your blinders and let's think of Fun Days. I'll think first. I'm a-thinkin' . . ."

In the dark room it was almost like being in a theater, waiting for the play to begin. And now Grandpa was drawing the curtain aside.

"I'm a-thinkin'," he began again, "back on Armed Forces

51

Day, and I'm a-ridin' little Misty in the big parade 'cause you two both got the chickenpox. Recomember?"

"Yes," they agreed politely. And for Grandpa's sake, Paul added, "Tell us about it."

"Why, I can hear the high-school band a-tootlin' and a-blastin' as plain as if 'twas yesterday. And all of 'em in blue uniforms with Chincoteague ponies 'broidered in gold on their sleeves. And now comes the Coast Guard, carryin' flags on long poles, marchin' to the music, and right behind 'em comes me and the firemen a-ridin'."

Now the children were caught up in the drama, reliving the familiar story.

"Misty, she weren't paradin' like the big hosses the firemen rode. She come a-skylarkin' along, and ever'where a little riffle of applause as she goes by. But all to once she seen a snake—'twas one of them hog-nose vipers—and 'twas right plumb in the middle of the street, and she r'ared up and come down on it and kilt it whilst all the cars in the rear was a-honkin' 'cause she's holdin' up the parade."

Grandpa stopped for breath. He gave the children a squeeze of mingled pride and joy. "Why, she was so riled up over that snake she like to o' dumped me off in the killin'. But I hung on, tight as a tick, and I give her a loose rein so's she could finish the job, and . . ."

Maureen interrupted. "Grandpa! You forgot all about our pup."

Grandpa winked at Grandma. His trick had worked. He had lifted the children out of their worry. "Gosh all fish-hawks," he chuckled, "I eenamost did. What was that little feller's name?"

52

"Why, Whiskers!" Maureen prompted.

" 'Course," Grandpa said, scratching his own whiskers as he remembered. "Well, that pup was a-ridin' bareback behind me, and when Misty r'ared, he went skallyhootin' in the air. But you know what? He picked himself up and jumped

53

right back on, after the snake-killin' was done. And Misty won a beautiful gold cup for bein' the purtiest and bravest pony in the hull parade."

"And that was even afore she became famous in the movie," Paul added.

Grandpa stopped, groping in desperation for another story. In the short moment of silence a gust of wind twanged the telephone wires and wailed eerily under the eaves.

Maureen's face went white. "Oh, Grandpa!" she whimpered. "Is Misty's baby going to die?"

"No, child. How often do I got to tell you I'm the oldest pony raiser on this here island, and if I know anything at all about ponies, Misty'll hold off 'til the storm's over and the sun's shinin' bright as a Christmas-tree ball."

Paul leaped from the couch. "Grandma!" he challenged. "Do *you* believe that?"

Grandma was putting away the last of the dishes, and did not reply. The question was so simple, so probing. She wanted to tell the truth and she wanted to calm the children. "As ye know," she said at last, "I had ten head o' children, and it seemed like *they* did the deciding when was the time to appear. But from what yer Grandpa says, ponies is smarter'n people. They kin hold off 'til things is more auspicious."

Grandpa brushed the talk aside. "I got another worriment asides Misty," he said. "She's safe enough on high ground and in a snug shed. But what about all my ponies up to Deep Hole?" He jerked up from the couch. "I got to call Tom Reed."

"Clarence," Grandma reproached, "Tom Reed's an early-to-bedder. Time we bedded down, too. It's past nine."

"I don't keer if it's past midnight," he cried in a sudden burst. "I *got* to call him!" But he didn't go to the phone. He suddenly stood still, his hands clenched into fists. "Somethin' I been meanin' to tell ye," he said with a kind of urgency.

No one helped him with a question. Everyone was too bewildered.

"All I know in this world is ponies. Ponies is my life," he went on. "And ever' Pony Penning I buy me some uncommon purty ones." Now the words poured from him. "Some fellers salt their money in insurance and such, but I been saltin' mine in ponies. And right now I got ninety head. And they're up to Deep Hole in Tom Reed's woods. I *got* to know how they are!"

"Ninety head!" Grandma gasped. "I had no idea 'twas so many."

"Well, 'tis." Grandpa's voice was tight and strained. "If the ocean swallers 'em, we're licked and done." He looked at the children. "And there'll be no schoolin' for this second brood o' ours." He rubbed the bristles in his ears, the worry in his face deepening. "One of the ponies is Wings."

"Oh . . . oh . . ." Maureen's lips trembled as if she had lost a friend. "Not Wings!"

"Not Wings!" Paul repeated.

"Who's Wings?" Grandma demanded.

"Why, Grandma," Paul said, "he's the red stallion who stole Misty away for two weeks last spring. Don't you remember? He's the father of Misty's unborned colt."

Maureen went over to Grandpa and took his gnarled old hand into hers and pressed it against her cheek. "Tonight I'm going to send up my best prayer for Wings. And for all ninety head," she added quickly. "But, Grandpa, we don't mind about school. Honest we don't."

" 'Course not," Paul said. "We'll just raise more ponies from Misty."

Chapter 6

OCEANUS

"TRY ONCET more, Lucy! Just oncet more!" Grandpa was imploring the operator.

Paul and Maureen were on the floor at Grandpa's feet, listening anxiously. Grandma brought in the lantern and set it on the organ near him as if somehow it would help them all hear better.

After an unbearable wait Grandpa bellowed, "Tom! That you, Tom? How are my ponies?"

A pause.

"What's that? You're worried about your son's *chickens!*" Grandpa clamped his hand over the mouthpiece and snorted in disgust. He summoned all of his patience. "All right, tell me 'bout the chickens, but make it quick." He held the receiver slightly away from his ear so that everyone could listen in.

"My son," Tom Reed was shouting as loud as Grandpa, "raises chickens up to my house, you know."

"Yup, yup, I know."

"He's got four chicken houses here, and he comes up about eight o'clock tonight, and wind's a-screeching and a-blowing, and the stoves burn more coal when the wind blows hard."

"I know!" Grandpa burst forth in annoyance. "But what about . . ."

"He puts more coal on and he asks me to help, and tide wasn't too far in then. But when we'd done coaling, he goes on back to his house. And an hour or so later he calls me up all outa breath. 'Tide's risin' fast,' he says. 'Storm's worsening. I can't get back up there. Will you coal the stoves for me?' So I goes out . . ."

Grandpa stiffened. "What'd ye find, Tom? Any o' my ponies?"

"All drowned."

A cry broke from the old man: "All ninety head?"

"They was all drowned, two thousand little baby chicks. They was sitting on their stoves like they was asleep. The water just come right up under 'em. I guess two-three gasps, and they was all dead."

"Oh." Grandpa held tight to his patience. He was sorry about the chickens, but he had to know about his ponies. He cleared his throat and leaned forward. "Tom!" he shouted. *"What about my ponies?"*

There was a long pause. Then the voice at the other end stammered, "I don't know, Clarence, but no cause to worry —yet. Stallions got weather sense. They'll just drive their mares up on little humpy places."

Grandpa wasn't breathing. His face turned dull red.

"They must of sensed this storm," the voice went on. "Tonight after I watered 'em, they just wanted to stay close to the house. But I drove 'em out to the low pasture like always. I'll go out later with my flashbeam. You call me back, Clarence."

There was a choking sound. The children couldn't tell whether it was Grandpa or a noise on the line.

"You hear me, Clarence? I'll go out now. Call me back."

Blindly Grandpa put the receiver in place. He went to the window and stood there, his head bowed.

No one knew what to say. Their world seemed to hang like a rock teetering on a cliff.

The quiet felt heavy in the room, with only the wind screaming. Suddenly Grandpa turned around. His eyes seemed to throw sparks. "Idy! Play something loud. Bust that organ-box wide open. March music, mebbe. Anything to drown out that wind. And Paul and Maureen, quit gawpin'. Get up off'n the floor and sing! Loud and strong. Worryin' won't do us a lick o' good."

Grandma was relieved to have something to do. She plumped herself on the organ bench, spreading out her skirt as if she were on the concert stage. "Now then," she turned to Grandpa, "I'll play 'Fling Out the Banner.' "

"I don't know the words," Paul said.

"Me either," Maureen chimed in.

"Ye can read, can't ye?" Grandpa barked. "Here's the song book. Go ahead now. I'll be yer audience."

The organ notes rolled out strong and vibrant, and the children sang lustily:

> "Fling out the banner, let it float
> Skyward and seaward, high and wide . . ."

When they were well into the second verse, Grandpa silently tiptoed into the hall, put on his gumboots and slicker, and let himself out into the night.

A flying piece of wood narrowly missed his head as he went down the steps, and a piece of wet pulpy paper hit him full in the face. He wiped it off and focused his light to see the path to the corral. But there was no path; it was covered by water. He drew his head into his coat and sloshed forward, bent double against the wind. "'Tain't a hurricane, it's naught but a full tide," he kept telling himself. "Still, I don't like it, with Misty so close to her time."

Inside the shed all was dry and warm. Misty was lying asleep, with Skipper back-to-back. The light brought the collie to his feet in a twinkling. He almost knocked Grandpa down with his welcome. Misty opened wide her jaws and yawned in Grandpa's face.

He couldn't help laughing. "See!" he told himself. "Nothing to worry about. Hoss-critters is far smarter'n human-critters." He fumbled in his pocket and found a few tatters of tobacco and said to himself, "Watch her come snuzzlin' up to me." And she did. And he liked the feel of her tongue on his hand and the brightness of her eye in the beam of his flashlight.

Affectionately he wiped his sticky palm on her neck and said, "I got to go in, Misty, now I know ye're all right. See you in the morning, and by then all the water'll slump back into the ocean where it b'longs."

When he came into the kitchen, Grandma was standing with a broom across the door. "Praises be, ye're safe!" she exclaimed. "I been holdin' these young'uns at bay. They wanted to follow ye."

"Grandpa! Has the colt come?" Maureen and Paul asked in one breath.

"Nope. And if I'm any judge, 'tain't soon. Now everybody to bed. Things is all right. We got to think that."

"Paul and I, we can't go to bed yet," Maureen protested.

"And why can't ye?"

"We haven't done our homework."

"Clarence," Grandma said, "you're all tuckered out, and you can't call Tom Reed 'cause our telephone's dead as a doorknob. So you go on to bed. I'll listen to the homework so's no more members of this household tippytoe out behind my back."

Grandpa patted everyone good night and went off, loosening his suspenders as he went.

"I feel like Abraham Lincoln studying by candlelight," Maureen said, bringing her pile of books close to the lantern.

"Wish you looked more like him," Paul teased, "instead of like a wild horse with a mane that's never been brushed."

"Humph, *your* hair looks like a stubblefield."

"Children, stop it!" Grandma interrupted. "Ye can have yer druthers. Either ye go to bed or ye get to work."

Paul weighed the choices, then reluctantly opened his

science book. But at the very first page he let out a whistle. "Listen to this! 'If the ancients had known what the earth is *really* like, they would have named it Oceanus, not Earth. Huge areas of water cover seventy per cent of its surface. It is indeed a watery planet.' "

"Now that's right interesting," Grandma said, putting a few sticks of wood into the stove.

"Yes," Maureen pouted, "a lot more interesting than trying to figure how many times 97 goes into 10,241."

Paul waxed to his lesson as a preacher to his sermon. "Listen! 'People used to say the tides were the breathing of the earth. Now we know they are caused by the gra-vi—gra-vi-ta—gra-vi-ta-tion-al pull of the moon and sun.' "

"I do declare!" Grandma said. "It makes my skin run prickly jes' thinkin' about it."

"Go on!" Maureen urged. "What's next?"

Paul read half to himself, half aloud. " 'When the moon, sun, and earth are directly in line—as at new moon and full moon—the moon's and the sun's pulls are added together and we have unusually high tides called spring tides.' "

Grandma sat rocking and repeating, "I declare! I do declare!" until her head nodded. Suddenly she jerked up and looked at the clock. "Paul Beebe! Stop! It's way past ten and, lessons or no, we all got to get to bed. *This instant!*"

Chapter 7

THE SEA TAKES OVER

ALL NIGHT long Paul heard the driving rain and the wind lashing the dead vine across his window. Even in his dreams he heard it. As gray daylight came, his sleepy voice kept mumbling, "They should've named it Oceanus . . . Oceanus . . . Oceanus."

His own words brought him awake. Scarcely touching his toes to the cold floor, he leaped to the window and pulled the curtain aside. He stared awestruck.

The sea was everywhere, all around. The tide had not ebbed. It had risen, its waves dirtied and yellowed by sand and jetsam. They were licking now against the underpinning of the house. Suddenly Paul knew it was more than rain he had heard in his dreams. It was the sea on its march to the house.

All at once fear was sharp in him, like a pain. Misty had drowned! She had drowned because she was trapped in a stall. He himself had bolted and locked and trapped her. If only, long ago, he had sent her back to Assateague with the wild things where she belonged! Then she could have climbed the White Hills and been saved. If only. . . . If . . . !

Angry at himself, almost blaming himself for the storm, he pulled on his blue jeans over his pajamas. And he yelled for Grandpa as he tore through the silent house to the back hall.

The old man was already there, struggling into his hip boots. "Shush! Shush!" he whispered. "You'll wake yer Grandma and Maureen. Ain't nothing they can do to help. Mebbe," his voice was tight and bitter, "ain't nothing anybody can do."

Paul hoped Grandpa wouldn't notice the tremble of his hands as he buttoned his jacket. But Grandpa was busy gathering up a pile of supplies—some old, worn bath towels, a thermos jug of hot water, a box of oatmeal, and a small brown paper sack. He stuffed the towels inside his slicker, picked up the jug, and gave the oatmeal and the sack to Paul.

"Mind you keep them dry," he cautioned. "The sack's got sugar inside . . . in case o' emergency."

He opened the door, and the old man and the boy stepped out into a terrifying seventy-five-mile-an-hour gale. The sudden pressure half-knocked Paul's breath out. The rain blew into his eyes faster than he could blink it away. He felt Grandpa thrust a strong arm through his, and linked tight together they flung themselves against the wind, floundering

ankle-deep in the choppy water. Paul's heart hammered in his chest and he cried inside, "Please, God, take the sea back where it belongs. Please take it back."

As they stumbled along, Grandma's new-hatched chicks swept by them and out to sea on the tide. And they saw two squawking hens, their feet shackled by seaweed, struggling to reach their chicks. But they were already out of sight. Paul and Grandpa, too, were helpless to save them.

Numb and weary, they reached the shed, and to their relief it was a windbreak. They caught their breath in its shelter. At least, Paul thought, the wind won't rush in when we open the door.

Grandpa set down his jug. Paul opened the door just a crack. Fearfully, uncertainly, they peered in. They stared unbelieving. Maureen, looking like a wet fish or a half-drowned mermaid, sat dozing on Misty's back. Skipper was sleeping at her feet, curled up in a furry ball.

As the door creaked on its hinges, Misty shied and Maureen fell off in a surprised heap. She bounced up like a jack-in-the-box.

"Wal, I never!" Grandpa clucked as he and Paul went inside. "Seems like we're intrudin'. Eh, Paul?"

Paul's surprise turned to resentment. "Least you could've done, Maureen, was to wake me up."

"And who usually goes off alone?"

"Who?"

"You! Remember when you sneaked Grandpa's boat and went to Assateague all alone?"

"Oh, that! That was no place for a girl."

"Stop it!" Grandpa shouted. He gave Maureen a gentle

spank, then turned to Paul. "We've got all the makings here. You and Maureen fix a hot mash for Misty. I'll wade over to the hay house and see to Watch Eyes and Billy Blaze and the mares. You two wait for me here."

Later, at breakfast, Paul started to tell Grandma about her chicks, but he couldn't bring himself to do it. She was spooning up the porridge, trying to hide her fears with nervous chatter. "As you said, children, there's a time to go to school and a time to stay home. Well, this-here is the time to stay home. I won't have you going out again and catchin' the bad pneumonia."

"Guess ye're right, Idy," Grandpa agreed.

Paul and Maureen merely nodded. For once, a holiday from school did not seem attractive. They ate in silence.

"I've a good mind to feed you sawdust after this," Grandma went on. "Not a one of ye would know the difference."

Halfway through, Grandpa pushed his bowl of porridge aside. "It's stickin' in my gullet," he said. He got up from the table and stood over the stove, flexing his fingers. "Any way ye look at it," he sighed heavily, "we're bad off. Our old scow tore loose in the night—it's gone. And likely our ninety head up to Deep Hole are gone, too." His body shivered. "But even so," he added quietly, "we're lucky."

Maureen sat up very straight. "You have me and Paul," she said solemnly.

"That's 'zactly what I mean! We got us two stout-built grandchildren, and they're not afeard to buckle down and pull alongside us."

Paul stood up. He felt strong and proud, as if he could tackle anything. "I'm going with you, Grandpa."

"How'd ye know I'm going anywheres? But I am! I got to get over to town. Human folk may need rescuin'."

Grandma's lips pressed into a thin line. "Ye can't go! There's no road! Water'd come clean up over your boots."

"There, there, Idy. The wind's let up some, and Billy Blaze and Watch Eyes is used to plowin' through water. If they can't walk, they kin swim. Boy, ye ready?"

Paul shot a look of triumph at Maureen and immediately felt ashamed.

"Clarence!" Grandma pleaded, trying to keep her menfolk at home. "I won't have you going off and over-straining yourself. You, and me too," she added quickly, "is getting agey. Besides, soon the telephone will come on, and the electric, and we can all set cozy-like and listen to the news on the radio."

"If everyone was to stay home, Idy, a lot of folk might go floatin' out to sea like yer baby chicks." He clapped his hand over his mouth. He hadn't meant to tell her. But now it was too late.

Grandma's eyes filled. She covered her face with her hands. "Pore little chickabiddies," she whispered, "with their soft yellow fuzz and their beady birdy eyes." She wiped her tears with her apron. "All right, go 'long," she said. "I just hope your herd up to Tom's pasture ain't met the same fate."

Grandpa put a gentle hand on her shoulder. "That's another reason I got to go," he said. "When I'm fightin' the elements, I can't be grievin' about my herd. If they've weathered the night, they'll last the day. And if they ain't . . ."

"I'll keep watch on Misty," Maureen offered. "And if there's any trouble, Grandma knows all about birthing."

Chapter 8

PAUL TO THE RESCUE

By THE TIME Paul and Grandpa set out on Watch Eyes and Billy Blaze, the wind had dropped to fifty miles an hour. Yet the water from the ocean was stealthily creeping up and up as if to reclaim this mote of land and take it back to the sea. Spilling and foaming, the tide continued to rise—flooding chicken farms, schoolyards, stores and houses—in its surge to join ocean and bay.

Watch Eyes and Billy Blaze were used to surf and boggy marsh, for they had been on many a wild pony roundup. Feeling ahead for footholds they pushed forward, step by step, not seeming to mind the water splashing up on their bellies.

Grandpa, on Blaze, cupped one hand about his mouth and yelled above the wind. "Turn off at Rattlesnake Ridge, Paul. We'll stop at Barrett's Grocery first and get the news."

Paul nodded as though he had heard. He was staring, horror-struck, at the neighbors' houses. Some had collapsed. And some had their front porches knocked off so they looked like faces with a row of teeth missing. And some were tilted at a crazy slant.

Anger boiled up in Paul—anger at the senseless brutality of the storm. He rode, shivering and talking to himself: "The big bully! Striking little frame houses that can't stand up to it, drubbing them, whopping them, knocking their props out."

A street sign veered by, narrowly missing the horses' knees. *98th Street,* it said. Grandpa turned around to make sure he had read it aright. "My soul and body!" he boomed. "It scun clean down from Ocean City! That's thirty mile away!"

Without warning, Watch Eyes suddenly slipped and went floundering. Paul's quick hand tightened on the reins, lifting his head. He felt Watch Eyes jolt, then stretch out swimming. "Go it! Go it!" he shouted, and he stood up in his stirrups, feeling a kind of wild excitement. This was like swimming the channel on Pony Penning Day. Only now the water was icier and it was spilling into his boots, soaking his blue jeans and the pajamas he still had on. Yet his body was sweating and he was panting when they reached the store.

In front of Barrett's Grocery two red gas pumps were being used as mooring posts for skiffs and smacks and trawlers. A Coast Guard DUKW, called a "duck," and looking

like a cross between a jeep and a boat, came churning up alongside Grandpa and Paul. The driver called out: "Mr. Beebe! We need you both." His voice was a command. "Tie up your horses in Barrett's barn and come aboard."

From under the tarpaulin a child's voice cried excitedly, "Paul, how's Misty?"

And another spoke up. "Has she had her baby yet?"

Paul shook his head.

Mr. Barrett's barn had a stout ramp, and Watch Eyes and Billy Blaze trotted up and inside like homing pigeons. After Paul and Grandpa had loosened the ponies' girths and slipped the bits under their chins, they waded out to the DUKW. The passengers squeezed together to make room. Then the DUKW turned and chugged toward the village.

"Sir!" Paul asked the driver. "Could you take us up to Deep Hole to see about Grandpa's ponies?"

Grim-faced, the man replied, "Got to save people first."

As they turned onto Main Street, which runs along the very shore of the bay, Paul was stunned. Yesterday the wide street with its white houses and stores and oyster-shucking sheds had been neat and prim, like a Grandma Moses picture. Today boats were on the loose, bashing into houses. A forty-footer had rammed right through one house, its bow sticking out the back door, its stern out the front.

Nothing was sacred to the sea. It swept into the cemetery, lifted up coffins, cast them into people's front yards.

Up ahead, a helicopter was letting down a basket to three people on a rooftop. Grandpa gaped at the noisy machine in admiration. "I itch to be up there," he shouted, "lifting off the old and the sick."

Paul too wanted to do big rescue work.

As if reading his mind, the driver turned to him. "Son," he said, "do you feel strong enough to save a life?"

"Yes, sir!"

"Good. You know Mr. Terry—the man who has to live in a rocking bed?"

Paul nodded. "It rocks by electric, but he's got a gasoline generator now. Mrs. Terry was telling Grandpa last night."

"Yes, but along about midnight the gas ran low. It took the firemen an hour to get through this surf to deliver more gas to keep the generator running. He's still alive . . ."

"Then what can I do?" Paul asked.

"Plenty, son. The whole island's running out of gas, and until helicopters can bring some in, that respirator's got to be worked by hand."

"Oh. 'Course I'll help."

The driver now turned to Grandpa. "These folks," he said, indicating his passengers, "are flooded out. We'll take them to the second story of the Fire House for shelter. Then we got to chug up to Bear Scratch section and rescue a family with six children. Whoa! Here we are at the Terrys'."

The DUKW skewered to a stop in front of a two-story white house.

"Good luck, Paul. When the gas arrives, grab any DUKW going by, and we'll meet you back at Barrett's Store along about noon."

Paul got out and plowed up to the house. The door opened as he stumbled up the flooded steps, and Mrs. Terry greeted him. Her face was pale, and there were deep circles under her eyes, but she smiled. "You've come to man the generator?"

"Yes, sir—I mean, yes, ma'am," Paul stammered. "I'm Paul Beebe."

"Oh," she smiled again. "So you're the Beebe boy. You're the one who rescued Misty when she was a baby and nearly drowned."

"Yes, ma'am."

"And to think that now she's going to have a baby of her own."

"Yes, ma'am. Any minute."

All the while she watched Paul pulling off his boots and jacket Mrs. Terry talked to him, but her head was cocked, ears alert, listening to the steady hum of the generator in the next room.

"We've so little gas left," she said. "The doctor says I'm to save it in case relief-men get worn out." She led the way down the hall to Mr. Terry's bedroom.

Paul blanched. Hospitals and sick rooms gave him a cold clutch of fear. But the moment he saw Mr. Terry smiling there in his rocking bed he was all eagerness to help. Maybe he could do a better job than an old machine. Maybe he could pump stronger and faster, so Mr. Terry'd get a lot more air in his lungs and his face wouldn't look so white.

Mrs. Terry showed Paul how to work the controls. "He's used to just twenty-eight rocks a minute," she explained. "No faster."

"Hi, son." The voice from the bed was weak but cheerful. "It's good of you to help."

Paul bent to his work, pushing up and down in steady rhythm, twenty-eight strokes to the minute. Maybe, he thought as the minutes went by, now I can qualify for a volunteer fireman. He was glad he was used to pumping water for the ponies. And that set him thinking of Misty, and the bittersweet worry rushed over him again so that he barely heard Mrs. Terry.

"How wonderful people are, Paul," she was saying. "With their property wrecked and their own lives endangered, they are so concerned about us. And we aren't even Chincoteaguers. We just came here to retire."

Paul heard the words far off. He was thinking: Sometimes newborn colts don't breathe right away and horse doctors have to pump air into their lungs with their hands—like this, like this, like this. Down, up, down, up, down, up. Would it be twenty-eight times a minute for a little foal? Or more? Or less? How would he know? Why hadn't he asked Dr. Finney, the veterinarian from Pocomoke?

Runnels and rivulets of sweat were trickling down his back; his face and hair were dripping as if he were still out in the rain.

"Paul!" Mrs. Terry was saying, "Look! A whole beautiful tank of gas has come. And the DUKW man is waiting to give you a ride back. High time, too. You're all tuckered out, poor lamb!"

Mr. Terry smiled and shook hands with Paul. "In my book, you are a hero," he said.

In Barrett's store the smell of fresh-ground coffee and cheese and chewing tobacco was mixed with the stench of wet boots and dead fish. Paul stepped inside and closed the door. Groups of men were standing, knee deep in water, gabbling to each other like long-legged shore birds. Paul waited by the door until Tom Reed beckoned him over.

"Yes, sir-r-r!" a man with a cranelike neck was saying, "I figure two, three pressure areas come together and made a kind of funnel."

Mr. Barrett was waiting on customers and listening at the same time. He leaned over the counter. "To my notion," he said, "this storm made a figure eight and come back again afore the tide ever ebbed."

Paul tugged at Tom's sleeve. "Mr. Reed," he whispered, "what about Grandpa's ponies up to your place?"

"Don't know, Paul. And we won't 'til we can get back into the woods. Water's too deep to walk in, and the DUKWs are too busy rescuin' people."

The storekeeper leaned across the counter, nosing in between Paul and Tom Reed. "Who's next, gentlemen?"

Paul felt in his pocket, counting his money. "I have thirty-nine cents," he said. "I can buy two cans of beans."

"If only we'd of got some notice of this storm," Mr. Barrett was saying as he spilled the coins into the drawer. "With a hurricane you know ahead, and when it's over, it's over."

"Yup," the men agreed. "A hurricane blows crazy, then it's gone. But a tidal storm sneaks up on you and stays."

Wyle Maddox, the leader of the roundup men, had been listening as he crunched on an apple. He came over now to Tom Reed. "Tom," he said, "you're blest with mother-wit. You're the one knows most about sea and sky. How do *you* figure it?"

The small, spare man blushed. "Pshaw, Wyle, I'm no authority, but as I see it, the storm looped and come back, and kept a-pressin' and a-pressin' the water into the bay instead of letting it go out at ebb time."

"But why is the water so high on the bay side nearer the mainland?"

" 'Cause usually it's a nor'west wind that helps the tide flow back out of the bay, but this time, wind blew nor'east and the water jes' swelled up into a bulge at the narrows, and it had to go somewheres."

The door suddenly opened, letting in the sound and cold of the wind, and with it came Grandpa Beebe, looking hale and ruddy alongside the lean fisherfolk.

"What's the news?" Mr. Barrett called out.

Grandpa looked from face to face. "Bad," he said. "Government's declared Chincoteague a disaster area."

A cry of scorn went up. "Disaster area? That's no news."

"But *this* is! A hull fleet of heelyacopters is comin' in from the military this afternoon and we're all supposed to e-vac-u-ate over to the main."

"*Evac*uate?" The word dropped like a time bomb. Then the explosion.

"Why?"

"What fer?"

"Mebbe okay for sick folk."

"Yeh. Or the homeless."

"Me, I got a second story."

"Me, too."

Everyone was talking at once. Everyone but Paul. He felt a hard lump in his stomach. He would refuse to go . . . unless they took Misty, too. The storekeeper rapped on the counter for silence. "Fellers, let's hear Mr. Beebe out."

Grandpa took a moment before he went on. "Tide's supposed to come up higher," he announced. "Four feet higher."

"*Four feet!* Why, that'll flood the whole island. Every house, every store. Even the Fire House and the churches!"

"But that's only half the reason. Government says there could be an epidemic of the typhoid, 'cause of all the dead chickens and fish a-rottin' and mebbe"—Grandpa avoided Paul's eyes—"mebbe dead ponies."

The talk ceased. There was a sudden exodus. Men sloshing heavy-footed out of the store, getting into their boats, going home to their families, figuring out how to break the news.

"Come, Paul," Grandpa beckoned.

Paul followed along. "I bought us two cans of beans," he offered, not knowing what to say.

"Ain't goin' to need 'em," Grandpa said gruffly; then he turned to look at Paul. "They might taste real good, though, come to think of it."

Chapter 9

WAITING FOR THE WHIRLYBIRD

GETTING HOME was rough going and agonizingly
slow. The horses plodded through the water when they could,
and swam when they had to. Paul and Grandpa stopped once
to let them blow. Then they pressed on, man and creature
eager for Home.

Almost there, Paul saw the higher ground of Pony Ranch
with the buildings still standing brave and whole—the cot-
tage, its green roof darkened by the rain, the made-over
chicken coop and the hay house and the smokehouse—but
they looked littler than before, and somehow frightened, with
the sea creeping up on them.

At the gate Grandpa made his decision. "Ride down to the smokehouse, Paul," he said. "Pick us out a big ham. If we got to go, we ain't showin' up over on the main empty handed. I'll dry off Billy Blaze and see about Misty."

Skipper swam out to meet Paul, then paddled alongside

all the way to the smokehouse. Round as a silo and perched on the highest spot of the ranch, the smokehouse was a landmark for ships in the channel. Inside, it was a friendly place, with its exciting smells, sweet and smoky. In the little while it took Paul to select the biggest ham and to cut a piece of rind for Skipper, the rain turned to icy sleet.

Grandpa was throwing an old red blanket over Misty

when Paul looked in. "Grandpa!" he cried. "Misty's standing in water!"

"So'm I!"

"But you're not going to have a colt!"

"Wisht I was. Then maybe I'd get a bit o' coddlin'.'"

"But, Grandpa! What are we going to do with her?"

"The only thing left to do."

"What's that?"

"Take her smack into the kitchen."

"Into *Grandma's kitchen?*"

"The very one. And that's where she's goin' to stay 'til tide ebbs."

"Whew! How're you going to ask her?"

"I ain't askin'. I'll jes' put her halter on and lead her up the steps and onto the porch and in through the door."

"No, I mean how you going to ask Grandma."

"O–h. I ain't askin' her, neither. I'll jes' tell her, quiet-like."

But Grandpa didn't tell her quietly. He led up to it like a growing storm. "Idy! Maureen!" he thundered as he and Paul stomped in. "Yer menfolk are home."

"Praised be the Lord!" Grandma exclaimed. "I been so worried I couldn't do a lick o' work. Just sat by the window praying double-quick time."

"Tell it now," Paul whispered to Grandpa.

"Now ain't the time."

"But Misty's feet are wet."

"Won't hurt her none. Salt water's good for feet, man or beast." He turned now to Grandma. "Idy, dear, don't set the table. We'll jes' stand up and eat beans and sop up the 'lasses with some of yer good bread. Then we got some packin' to do, Idy dear."

Grandma mimicked. "Don't you 'Idy-dear' me, Clarence Beebe! What you up to? Yer face is red as a gobbler's wattle."

Paul giggled nervously. Often he had thought their tom turkeys and Grandpa looked alike, but he had never dared say it. He couldn't stop giggling. And soon Maureen was laughing along with him.

Grandma began to chuckle without knowing why. "I declare to goodness! Hearing people laugh is like sunshine flooding the house."

"It's floodin' I want to talk to ye about, Idy."

The laughter stopped.

Grandpa's voice was stern. "All morning heelyacopters been carryin' off the sick. Now they're comin' for folks as is well."

"Not me, they ain't!" Grandma flared up. "They can jes' count me out! I'm too old to start riding acrost the sky in an eggbeater."

"All righty! Mebbe ye prefers stayin' here and havin' sharks and crabs slinkin' into yer house and grabbin' ye." He winked at the children. "Recomember the day when that crab pinched yer Grandma when she was bendin' over, gatherin' oysters? Why, she went off like one o' them big rockets from Wallops Beach."

Grandma turned her back and began slicing bread with a vengeance.

"But what'll happen to Misty?" Maureen asked in alarm.

"*I'll* stay with Misty," Grandma announced without turning around. "Much as I dislikes treating ponies like folks, I admit to a kinship when she's having a baby."

Grandpa cut open the can of beans with his knife. "Paul," he growled, "mebbe *ye* can explain things to yer Grandma."

"It's true, Grandma," Paul said, helping himself to the heel of bread. "Tide's coming back four foot higher, and the island's going to be contamin—going to be spoilt rotten with dead chickens and stinky fish and snakes and mushrats and maybe even dead horses." He looked at Grandpa, wishing he hadn't said that. Then he went on quickly. "Health officials want everybody to clear out. They say there could be a fierce epidemic."

No one spoke. Grandma sat down at the table and stared vacantly. She brushed imaginary crumbs into her hand.

"Wa–al, Idy," Grandpa said, "ye can have yer druthers. Do ye want to stay and take a chance on losin' Paul and Maureen to the typhoid? Or do ye want to light out now, afore the tide pushes us out?"

For the first time Grandma began to waver. "Why, I had no idea 'twas that bad, Clarence."

"Wal, 'tis! Way to look at it is: people *got* to go. Why, up to the north end of the island there was one big fat lady, weighed nigh two hundred pound, and this lady and her teen-age girl and her girl's beau was a-sittin' in their house just talkin' away, and all to once a big whoosh o' the sea come spang into their sittin' room, and they was scramblin' atop tables and chairs, and they would've clumb into the attic if they'd a had one. But they didn't. An' that young boy, he had to saw a hole in their ceilin', mind ye, and he clumb up into the teensy air space there under the roof, and with him a-pullin' and the girl a-pushin' they squeezed the mother up through the hole." Grandpa stopped for breath.

"What happened to them?" Maureen asked. "Were they there all night?"

"Yup, and 'long 'bout daybreak the boy sawed a hole in the roof and they all clumb out, and later one o' them whirly-birds come down and rescues the three o' them from the roof-top, all shivery and wet and hungry.

"Now, Idy, how'd ye like it if we had to cut a hole in our purty green roof, and I'd have to haul ye up like a sack o' potatoes?"

Paul nudged Grandpa. "Tell her now."

"So ye see, Idy, we could be next. Already flood waters is seepin' into Misty's stable. She's comin' into yer kitchen," he announced, "and that's where she's going to stay 'til the tide's out."

"Good heavings!" Grandma looked beaten.

"Now then," Grandpa went on heartily, "ye better start packing. We'll want a blanket apiece and we're takin' a beautiful ham to surprise the mainlanders. And speakin' o' eatin', these beans is Paul's treat."

At last Grandma accepted the truth. She began to scurry about, talking to herself. "We got to take some soap for sure, and we'll have to have a comb and . . ."

Grandpa and the children left her to her bustling. There was much to be done before the helicopter came. Misty had to be brought into the kitchen and, before that, the marsh ponies in the hay house had to be made comfortable.

"Let's lift down the top bales," Grandpa directed when

they reached the long shed. "We'll pile 'em two deep over the hull floor. That way even their feet'll be dry."

"And if we don't break open the bales," Paul said, "it'll take them just that much longer to eat the hay."

"They could live for a week in here," Maureen said.

" 'Zackly!" Grandpa nodded. "No need to worry 'bout them."

Then it was Misty's turn. Paul had expected to lead her out of her stall quietly and that she would foot her way along carefully, as any broodmare should. But the moment he put on her halter, she began quivering as if the wind and waves called up the wildness in her. Her head went up, her tail went up, her ears pricked sharply. And even in the bitter cold she broke out in sweat.

"Whoa there, girl, whoa," Paul soothed. He slid his hand through her halter as he opened her door. But with one leap she was in the water, lifting him off his feet. She didn't want

to be led. She wanted to splash and play like any Chincoteague pony.

Grandpa grabbed her from the other side. "Maureen!"
he yelled, "you hop on and ride her to the steps. Me and
Paul'll guide her from behind."

Maureen climbed aboard. Through her legs she could
feel Misty's heart pounding. The water was up to Misty's knees.
Then a swirl of it hit her belly. She tried to jump over it.

Maureen grabbed a handful of mane. "Yahoo!" she
cried in startled surprise.

Misty tried one more leap, then settled down and went
steadily forward. She reached the steps well ahead of Paul
and Grandpa, who came wading up, out of breath.

"Now here's the touchy part," Grandpa panted. "Steps're
mighty slippy and we don't want her fallin' and hurtin'
herself."

But Misty had been up these steps before. She clomped
up happily, lifting each foot high. On the top step she paused,
mesmerized. A little brown rabbit sat stock-still on the porch
rail, not a whisker twitching. It seemed more statue than real.
The two creatures stared at each other, the big soft brown eyes
and the small beady ones. Misty snorted as if to say, "What
you doing here? Go on back to your briar patch!" But the
rabbit never budged, not even when Misty stretched out her
neck and breathed right in its face.

Grandpa guffawed. Even then the cheeky little thing
stood its ground, more afraid of the rising water than of people or ponies.

"He's sassing Misty," Paul laughed. " 'Don't eye me,
ma'am,' he's saying, 'I been flooded out. Same as you.' "

90

At last Misty grew bored and ambled across the porch, through the back hall, and right into the kitchen. When they were all crowded inside, Grandpa took off his hat in a sweeping bow. "Meet Idy, my wife," he said.

Grandma winced. "We met before," she said drily. Then her heart melted. "Take off yer purty red shawl, Misty," she said, entering into the game, "and make yerself to home." She went to the refrigerator while Misty followed after, snatching a streamer of her apron.

Grandma jumped in fright, almost stumbling over her apron on the floor. "Why, that ungrateful rascal! I've a good notion to put these carrots back in the box." But she didn't. She held them out and let Misty lip them. "Feels tickly, her lips and whiskers, don't they?"

Paul and Maureen exchanged glances.

Grandma stiffened. "You're all dripping pools of water on my clean floor." She sighed. "But no matter now, I guess. How soon will the heelyacopter come for us?" she asked.

"Right soon," Grandpa replied. "Come on, son, we better hurry and haul in plenty of straw for Misty."

After they had made a deep rustly bed for her in the kitchen, there was nothing left to do. Four blankets and the ham were ready and waiting, and Misty was already at home, contentedly munching wisps of hay while Maureen combed her mane.

As the minutes dragged on, Grandma grew pale and fidgety. She busied herself pouring an extra bowl of milk for Wait-a-Minute. Then she began watering her sweet potato vine and her fern.

"That's my girl," Grandpa came over and patted her

shoulder. "That's my girl." Then he broke into a sudden howl as he caught her wetting down a plant of artificial violets.

Even Grandma laughed at herself and her color came back. "Believe now I'll just sit down and play us a hymn," she said. "I hate waiting for anything, 'specially heelyacopters."

She opened up the organ and began playing and singing. Her voice quavered at first, then grew stronger as if she wanted to reach God in his heaven, direct.

> "*Je*-sus, *Sav*-iour, *pi*-lot *me,*
>   *O*-ver *life's* tem-pest-uous *sea;*
>   *Un*-known *waves* be-fore me *roll,*
>   *Hi*-ding *rock* and treach-erous *shoal;*
>   *Chart* and *com*-pass *come* from *Thee;*
>   *Je*-sus, *Sav*-iour, pi-lot *me.*"

"That's great, Idy. Misty's ears is keeping time, turning ever' which way."

Then Grandpa saw the helicopter breaking through the dun-colored sky. "Play it once more," he urged. "Just once more!" No use worrying her too soon, he thought.

Again Grandma's trembly voice filled the little house.

> "*Je*-sus, *Sav*-iour, *pi*-lot *me,*
>   *O*-ver *life's* tem-pest-uous *sea.*"

Chapter 10

BACKYARD LANDING

THE HELICOPTER was chewing into the wind, coming closer and closer to Pony Ranch. Almost over the house it stopped in midair, engine roaring. It silenced even Grandma's music.

Everyone flew to the window, including Misty. They watched as the noisy machine hung over their heads.

"He's trying to decide!" Paul yelled.

"Who is? What?" Maureen wanted to know.

"The pilot, silly. He's figuring out where to land."

Grandpa was spellbound. "Ain't that beautiful? It's hangin' in the air jes' like a hummer-bird."

"Oh, mercy me!" Grandma cried as the helicopter tilted drunkenly, and began a steep vertical descent. "Oh . . . oh! It's going to set right in my daffydil bed!"

Like a bird aiming for its nest, the helicopter hovered over the mounded-up flower bed, then squatted down on the tiny patch.

Grandma watched in dismay as its rotors spit sand and water in every direction. She hid her face in her hands. "Oh, Clarence! Oh, Clarence!" she sobbed. "I can't go. I can't!"

"And why can't ye?" Grandpa demanded.

"Because, because . . ." She groped for a reason. "Misty'll ruin my linoleum and . . ." Here the sobbing became a wail, ". . . she'll chew on my nice new table with the let-down leaves."

"No, she won't!" Paul was on the defensive. "I'll stay and watch her."

"You listen to me, Paul Beebe," Grandpa exploded. "Anybody stayin' behind'll be me, head o' the household. Quick now! Everybody grab a blanket. I'll go out and explain things to that pilot." He started for the door.

Grandma reached it first and made a barricade of herself. Her crying was done. "If'n you stay behind, Clarence, we all do. Either we go as a fambly or we stay as a fambly."

Grandpa sighed, half amused, half annoyed. "Then everything's settled. Throw yer mind outa gear, Idy, and get yer duds on."

While Grandma was struggling into her overboots, Grandpa and the children were doing last-minute chores: opening a window from the top, just a crack, taking vegetables from the refrigerator and scattering them in amongst Misty's hay. Last of all, Grandpa put the stopper in the sink and turned on the cold water. "Makes a neat water trough, eh?" he chuckled, avoiding Grandma's eyes.

"You think she can manage without us?" Maureen asked.

"We got to think that, honey. And even if the tide seeps in, I made this straw bed so thick the little colt won't even get his hinder wet."

"Sure," Paul added. "And see how Wait-a-Minute is cozying up to Misty. They'll keep each other company. And see how calm she is, watching that 'copter. She's saying, 'I've seen big birds flapping their wings before.' "

"Oh, Paul, I wish I could read critters' minds the way you do."

"That's easy, Maureen. You just got to be smart as them."

Mr. Birch, the Coast Guard man, welcomed the Beebes at the foot of the stairs. Standing there in the water he looked like a preacher, ready to baptise his flock. "Wisht everybody was prompt, like you folks," he said as he herded them toward the helicopter, "and willing to cooperate without arguin'."

"We did all that afore you came," Maureen said.

Mr. Birch laughed. "Leave it to the young'uns to come out with the truth!" He helped Grandma up the steps and into the shuddering plane. "See, Mrs. Beebe, it's easier than boarding a train."

Maureen started to follow but suddenly turned to Paul, and almost in unison they let out one cry. "Skipper! Skipper!" They both called frantically. "S–k–i–p–p–e–r!"

Mr. Birch was shaking his head. "Sorry, children. We just have room for folks on this trip. All dogs stay behind."

"Put him in the kitchen, too," Grandma offered.

"Skipper! Here, Skipper!" The children whistled and screamed. But there was no sign of him. Only the water swirling, and the trees bending with the wind.

"All aboard!" the pilot called out. "We got another pick-up to make before dark. All aboard!"

Likely Skipper's drowned, Paul thought but didn't say aloud. He got into the helicopter and took a seat where he could look out at the house. But he refused to look.

"Fasten your seat belts!" the pilot ordered.

"Now, ain't this excitin'?" Grandpa yelled, as the blades overhead began whirring madly and the helicopter rose slowly off the earth and climbed straight up and up. "It's just like bein' in a elevator."

Grandma shook her head. She leaned toward the earth. taking a long last look at Pony Ranch, saying good-bye to it. Grandpa squeezed her hand comfortingly, and he looked down, too, down at the little house growing smaller and smaller.

"Such a racket!" Maureen cried. "Sounds faster than we're going."

Grandma held her hands over her ears. "Feels as if a thousand dentists are drilling inside my head."

"On your store teeth?" Paul grinned.

"Oh, Paul, stop teasing. I wish . . . I wish you and Maureen was littler. If only I had a baby to hold, I'd feel braver."

Grandma soon got her wish. At the next stop they picked up the Hoopers and the Twilleys and young Mrs. Whealton with her squalling baby. Just as the father of the baby was about to board, the pilot poked his head out the window. "Sorry, sir. We're full. You'll have to wait for the next one."

Quickly the young man tried to hand in a pile of diapers, but a gust of wind tore most of them away and they went flying off like kites.

Mrs. Whealton, clutching her baby, started to get out. "Stay put, lady. Everybody! Stay put!"

"I'll be along soon," Mr. Whealton called. And before the door closed, he thrust in the remaining diapers and the baby's bottle.

As the helicopter took off, Mrs. Whealton began sobbing louder than her baby. The passengers looked at one another, helpless and embarrassed. All except Grandma. She opened wide her arms.

"You just hand that little tyke acrost to me," she smiled, "and wipe yer eyes. You kin busy yerself foldin' the few diapers you got left."

Willingly Mrs. Whealton passed the baby across the aisle and into experienced hands. The crying stopped at once.

The northeast wind shook the helicopter, but it obeyed the pilot's stick. "We take no back talk from the elements," Mr. Birch said to reassure his passengers.

The plane was heading into the wind, flying low over the channel and over the long rib of sand that was Assateague. Everyone scanned the hills and woods for wild ponies.

"I see a bunch!" Paul cried.

"I knowed it! I knowed it!" Grandpa exulted. "They're atop the White Hills."

The pilot tried to hold the plane steady, but the gale buffeted it mercilessly. Twice he circled the herd, then climbed and headed due west. The island of Assateague seemed to be sailing backward, and now they were over Chincoteague again.

"Mr. Birch!" Maureen shouted. "Look at the people on that raft. They're waving a white flag."

"I see it," Mr. Birch answered, "but it's a housetop, not a raft, and they're waving a bedsheet. They don't know we got a full load."

From the cockpit the pilot called back, "We'll get 'em on the next trip. No, we won't!" he contradicted. "I see another chopper heading this way. They'll beat us to it."

Mr. Hooper, a quiet little man, said his first words of the trip. "Sky's so full o' whirlybirds we're goin' to need a traffic cop up here."

In spite of all the tragedy, the passengers couldn't help smiling at Mr. Hooper's joke.

"Yup," Grandpa agreed. "I can eenamost see a policeman mounted on a cloud like a parson in a pulpit."

But the make-believe fun didn't last. Now they were over the big bay of water, and now they could see the wavy shore of the mainland. Slowly the helicopter came down from the sky onto a landing field at Wallops Station. A thin fog was closing in and the night lights were already on as the Beebes and Hoopers and Twilleys and Mrs. Whealton tumbled out of the plane like seeds from a pod. A gust of wind swept them into a little huddle.

Suddenly the adventure and excitement were over. Standing there in the rain, Paul felt what he was, a refugee, homeless and cold and hungry. And half his mind was far away in a hay-strewn kitchen.

Chapter 11

REFUGEES

WALLOPS STATION is on the mainland of Virginia, just across the bay from Chincoteague Island. Once it had been a Naval Air Station, teeming with activity—planes roaring off and gliding in; signal crews waving orders; officers and men, pilots and engineers, radio technicians and clerks all criss-crossing from building to building. Then the government closed the base, and for three years the buildings stood empty, like a forest of dead trees.

But when the helicopter landed that stormy March evening, lights were blazing in every window. The whole place had come to life. Fire trucks were racing to meet helicopters, rushing sick refugees to the emergency hospital and others to the barracks and even the administration building.

The storm was now twenty-four hours old. Wind still blowing strong. Rain gusty. Clouds low. No moon, no stars.

At the edge of the landing strip the little clump of passengers stood huddled, clutching their blankets, staring at the yellow headlights coming toward them.

"Which building?" a fireman called out as he drove the truck within earshot.

Grandpa Beebe shouted back, "Don't know. Be there a fire?"

The driver replied with a boom of laughter, "There's no fire, Old Timer. I simply got to ask each family if they want to go where their friends are. Climb in, folks."

"Hey, Chief," Grandpa addressed the driver, "we don't any of us know one building from t'other. But if it's all the same to you, it'd be best to see to little Mis' Whealton first. In that shawl she's got the teensiest baby you 'most ever see."

The driver nodded. "Good idea," he said, backing and turning and roaring away. He dropped Mrs. Whealton and her baby at the hospital, left the Hoopers and the Twilleys at one of the barracks, and took the Beebe family to the mess hall. "There's more children here," he explained.

Wet and weary, Grandpa and Grandma, Paul and Maureen climbed the flight of stairs to the second floor, clutching their blankets. Paul still had the ham, now slung over his shoulder. An arrow on the wall pointed to an open door down the hall. Light streamed out and voices buzzed.

The room, half filled with refugees, was large and bright, and it smelled of wet wool and rubber boots, and fear and despair.

"Make yourself to home," an earlier arrival greeted them. "Just find a little spot to call your own. Lucky thing you have blankets. These floors are mighty hard for sleeping."

For a moment the Beebes stood looking around, trying to accustom their eyes to the light. Benches were lined up against the walls and scattered throughout the room. Most of the people were strangers to them, refugees from Nag's Head probably, or other islands nearby. They sat paralyzed, like animals caught in a trap, not struggling any more, just numbed. Only their eyes moved toward the entrance as each new family trudged in.

"They all look sad and full of aches," Grandma said, searching for a place to sit down.

"I see an empty bench," Maureen called, and led the way in and out among suitcases and camp chairs and children.

An old grizzled seaman in a ragged jacket came over and confronted Grandpa. He swore loud oaths to sea and sky. "Can't believe it could happen here," he said, pounding his fist on his hand. "Why, ye read 'bout it elsewheres . . ."

"Yeah. Tidal waves slam up in faraway places, but you never dream about it happening here."

At the far end of the room women from the Ladies' Aid were bringing in platters of sandwiches and a huge coffee pot.

"Take our ham over to them, Paul," Grandma said. "Mebbe they'd like to cut it in chunks and bake it with potatoes for tomorrow. I'd feel a heap happier if I could help," she confided to Maureen.

When the table was readied, people began forming in line. And all at once they were no longer trapped animals. They were human beings again, smiling at one another, sharing stories of rescue. Drawn by the smell of food, a long-eared pup shot out of a blanket and ran toward the table, his mistress after him.

Paul and Maureen joined the chase. "How'd you do it? How could you bring your dog?" Paul asked.

"Why, he's all the family I got, and I just rolled him up in his blanket. This afghan is really his," the woman explained, "and he burrowed into it like a turtle in his shell. The pilot didn't even see him. Tonight," she added with a smile, "he's got to share his blanket with me, for a change."

Maureen admired the dog, thinking of Skipper. "We couldn't find our Skipper," she said as she stroked and petted the little pup.

The lady was all sympathy. "Tell me about your dog."

"We had a big collie right up until time to leave," Paul answered.

"And we got a pony in our kitchen back in Chincoteague," Maureen spoke up.

The woman seemed suddenly to recognize Paul. "Why,

you're the boy who caught a wild mare over to Assateague and set her free again."

The children nodded.

"And the pony in your kitchen—is it Misty?"

"Yes, ma'am, it's Misty, all right."

The woman was excited. "Why, they been talking about her on the radio. Children who saw her movie are swamping the stations with calls, wanting to know if she drowned."

"She's safe," Paul said. "That is, she . . ." He stopped. He could feel his heart throbbing in his ears. In a split-second dream he was back on Chincoteague with the ocean rolling and pounding in under the house, and with a horrible hissing sound it was breaking the house apart, and in the same

instant Misty was swept out to sea until her mane became one with the spume. Paul shook off the dream as the woman called three young children to her.

"You youngsters," she said, "will be glad to know that Misty's safe in the Beebes' kitchen. And this is Paul and Maureen Beebe."

Wide-eyed, the children pelted them with questions. In the pain of uncertainty Paul answered what he could. Then he turned away, pulling Maureen along back to their bench. Grandma put an arm around each of them. "More folks are coming in," she said, trying to put their world back together. "Now mebbe we'll get some heart'ning news."

In a daze Paul and Maureen listened to the bits and pieces of talk.

"Old Dick Evans died trying to save his fish nets. Got plumb exhausted. His heart give out."

"When we flew over, I saw how the waves had chawed big chunks out of the causeway, and six autos were left, half-buried in sand. Even one of the DUKWs was stuck."

"When *we* flew over, the sea had swallowed up the causeway. Why, Chincoteague is cut off from the main like a boat without an anchor."

"I heerd that a lady over to Chincoteague had a husband and two children that couldn't swim. She swum two blocks in that icy water for help. Nearly died afore one of them DUKWs fished her up and drug her, sobbin' and drippin', to the Fire House. Then they goes back for her husband and kids." The speaker paused. "But guess what?"

"What?" someone asked.

"Why, between whiles a whirlybird airlifted 'em off'n the

roof and they thought *she'd* drownt and she thought *they'd* drownt. And later they all got together at the Fire House."

"See, children," Grandma whispered, "some of the news is right good."

A young reporter carrying his typewriter joined the gathering. "I heard," he said, "that a hundred and fifty wild ponies were washed right off Assateague."

"O–h!" The news was met by a shocked chorus.

"Before I write that for my paper, I'd like you folks to give me your comments." He took out a notebook and pencil.

A strained silence followed. The reporter looked around at the tight faces and put his notebook away.

Then the talk began again.

"I s'pose we oughtn't be thinking about wild ponies when people are bad off," a white-haired woman said.

"But what would it mean to Chincoteague," the reporter asked, "if Pony Penning Day had to be stopped for lack of ponies?"

Grandpa Beebe roused up. "Why, Chincoteague has took her place with the leading towns of the Eastern Shore. And mostly it's the wild pony roundup did it."

"That's what I say," a chorus of voices agreed.

"And if we had to stop it," Grandpa went on, "Chincoteague and Assateague both would be nothin' but specks on a map."

The reporter scribbled a few notes. Then he looked up. "Any of you hear about the man swept out to sea on a dining-room table while his wife accompanied him on the piano?"

His joke met with grim silence. It was too nearly true to be funny.

Grandma tugged at Grandpa's sleeve. "Clarence," she said, "we been hearing enough trouble. You tell the folks 'bout me and my violet plant."

Grandpa forced himself to smile. For the moment he put the worry aside. "Folks," he said, "my Idy here commenced waterin' her plants afore we took off. She give 'em a right smart nip. And then, split my windpipe if she didn't wet down the artyficial violet the kids give her for Christmas. She even saucered the pot to catch the come-through water, and dumped that in too!"

A young woman laughed nervously. "I can match that story," she offered. "The sea kept coming in under our door and kept pushing up my little rug, and I took my broom and tried to whisk it away, and then I got my dustpan and tried to sweep the water into it! A broom and a pan against the sea!"

A man, looking sheepish, said, "I tried the same stunt in my barn, only I used a shovel and a wheelbarrow!"

The talk petered out. Then a minister got up and prayed for a good night's sleep and for the tide to ebb and the wind to die. Gradually the people went back to their benches. One by one the lights were switched off, except for the night lights over the doors.

As the Beebes settled down in their corner, Grandpa whispered, "Close your eye-winkers, chirren, turn off your worries, and snore away the night." Then he got down on the floor, wrapped himself up like an Indian, and began breathing in deep, rhythmic snores.

"What better lullaby?" Grandma sighed.

And Paul and Maureen caught his calm, and they too slept.

Chapter 12

WAIT-A-MINUTE COULDN'T

BY SIX O'CLOCK the next morning the men had been outside summing up the weather, and had come in to report: "Wind's slacked up a bit. Still blowin' nor'nor'east. Sky's cloudy, but no rain."

By seven o'clock a new parade of church ladies marched in with big pans of sweet rolls and pots of steaming hot coffee.

At eight o'clock a Coast Guard officer, square-jawed and handsome, strode into the room. He was a big man, and when he pounded for order, the few leftover rolls jumped on their plates. "Folks," he boomed out, "I've good news for you." He waited a moment until his scattered audience finished folding their blankets and quieted down. "You'll be pleased to know," he announced, "that the Red Cross is coming in, bringing canned goods and a steam table so you can have nice hot meals."

One of the church ladies walked out in a huff.

"And they are bringing cots and pillows, so there'll be no more sleeping on the floor."

A shocked silence followed. Who wanted to stay another night? Even on a cot? Everyone wanted to get home.

"Bear in mind, friends," the brisk voice went on, "this is not a one-day evacuation. More refugees will be coming in."

"Where'll we put 'em?" several voices demanded.

The officer ignored the interruption. "By order of the State Department of Health, no women or children can return to Chincoteague until all the dead chickens are removed and the other carcasses, too—goats, dogs, pigs, and of course dead ponies. There could be a plague—typhoid or worse."

Grandpa's arms seemed big enough to take in his whole family. "Don't listen at the man. Ponies got sense. They'll hie theirselves to little hummocky places and wait it out. And Misty, of course, is dry and comfortable."

The officer let the mumblings and grumblings die down. He rapped again for silence. "The Mayor of Chincoteague has asked for volunteers—only able-bodied men—to fly back each day to clean up the island and repair the causeway. Only able-bodied men," he repeated, scrutinizing the group. "Will all who wish to volunteer come to the front of the room."

Grandpa leaped forward as if he'd been shot from a cannon. Paul was a quick shadow behind him.

"Paul Beebe!" Grandma called out. "You come back!"

But Paul seemed not to hear. He locked step with Grandpa and they were almost the first to reach the officer.

Grandma sighed. "Who can stop a Beebe? We can be proud of our menfolk, can't we, Maureen?"

Maureen burst into tears. "Oh, Grandma, being a girl is

horrible. Paul always gets to have the most excitement. And he'll be first to see Misty's baby. Oh, oh . . . ." And she buried her head in Grandma's bosom and sobbed.

"There, there, honey. We'll find something real interesting for you to do. You'll see."

A handful of lean, weathered fishermen were now lining up as volunteers. The officer began counting from the tail of the line. As he came to Paul, he stopped, trying to make up his mind if he were man or boy. For the moment he left Paul out and went on with his counting, ". . . eleven, twelve, thirteen, fourteen." At fourteen he paused.

"But, sir!" Paul heard his own voice sounding tight and urgent. "The 'copter holds fifteen, and Grandpa needs me. Don't you, Grandpa?"

The officer turned inquiringly to the old man.

"Fact is," Grandpa said proudly, "when it comes to handlin' livestock he's worth ten men."

"That settles it," the officer smiled. "We've completed our first load."

When the helicopter set down on Chincoteague right beside the Fire House, the Mayor was waiting for them, standing in the cold and the wet, slapping his hands together for warmth. He poked his head inside the cabin, quickly studied the occupants, then clipped out his orders: "Split into three bunches, men. Beebe, you and Paul go up to Deep Hole to check on the dead ponies and mark their location for removal by airlift. Charlie and Jack, you arrange for crews to pile up the dead chickens at convenient loading points. We'll need the rest of you to work on the causeway so's we can truck the chickens across. Thank you, men, for volunteering."

Three DUKWs were parked alongside the helicopter waiting to take each group to its base of operation. The driver of the first one beckoned Grandpa and Paul aboard with a welcoming smile. "You men are lucky," he said, "your house is okay; at least it was last time I was down there."

"Is . . . uh . . ." Paul stopped, embarrassed. The Coast Guardsman had just called him a man, and now he was frightened to ask a question, and more frightened not to ask.

"What you lookin' so scairt about?" Grandpa wanted to know.

"I want to ask him a question," Paul said miserably.

"Go ahead!" the driver encouraged as he steered through the debris-clogged street. "Go ahead."

Holding his breath, Paul blurted, "Is Misty all right? Has she had her colt?"

"Sorry, Paul, we been too busy to look in on her. But Mayor says I can take you there before we go up to Deep Hole."

It was strange, chugging down Main Street. Paul knew he ought to have remembered how it was from yesterday. But yesterday Chincoteaguers were sloshing along in hip boots, or

riding horses or DUKWs, and they were trying their best to joke and laugh. Today there were no home-folk faces. Grim soldiers were patrolling the watery streets, rifles held ready.

"What they here for?" Paul asked.

"To prevent looting," the Coast Guardsman replied.

But what's there to loot, Paul wondered, looking at the houses smashed like match boxes, with maybe only a refrigerator showing, or a bathtub filled with drift.

They passed other DUKWs plying up and down, delivering food to the Fire House, to the Baptist Church, to the few houses on higher ground where owners had refused to leave. And they passed heaps of rubble which once were old

landmarks—the oyster-shucking house, and the neat white restaurant whose owner boasted he bought his toothpicks by the carload. Now there was not even a toothpick in sight.

As the DUKW headed eastward to the spit of land that was Beebe's Ranch, Paul winced. The pretty sign, "Misty's Meadow," was still standing, but it didn't fit the spot. There was no meadow at all. Only a skim of murky yellow water.

Paul felt a strangling fear. He had waited all night and half the morning to see Misty. Now in sight of the house, he couldn't wait another moment. He started to jump out.

Grandpa put a restraining arm across his chest. "Ye're jerky as a fish on a hot griddle, son. Simmer down. Ponies can't abide fidgety folk."

After what seemed an eternity but was only a minute, the DUKW jolted to a stop and Paul and Grandpa were out and up the steps.

Breathless, Paul opened the door a crack, and all in a split second his worry fell away. Misty was whinkering as if she too had waited overlong for this moment, and she started toward him, but stepping very carefully, lifting her feet high, avoiding something dark and moving in the straw.

"My soul and body!" Grandpa clucked, looking over Paul's shoulder. "Ee-magine that!"

Then he and Paul were on their knees, and Paul was laughing weakly as he stroked Wait-a-Minute and admired her litter of four squirming, coal-black kittens.

"Ee-magine that!" Grandpa repeated. "Misty's postponed hers, but Wait-a-Minute couldn't!"

"A whole mess of kittens in Grandma's kitchen!" Paul said. Disappointed as he was, he couldn't help laughing.

114

Chapter 13

UP AT DEEP HOLE

AFTER HE had poked and felt of Misty, Grandpa threw up his hands in despair. "Could be a week yet."

Paul groaned, wondering if maybe the foal was dead inside her and that was why it wouldn't come out, wondering if she was really going to have a colt at all.

"Yup," Grandpa said, "mebbe she's goin' to wait till her stall dries out. She's still got plenty hay, so you feed the cat, whilst I take a quick gander about the house."

As Grandpa hurried down the hall, Paul searched the refrigerator. He took out the pitcher of milk and smelled it. "Phew-eee!" he said to himself. "She'll just have to be satisfied with the left-over beans."

Grandpa soon came back, rubbing his hands. "Water seeped into only one bedroom," he announced. "But the rooms is colder'n a tomb, and they stink like old fish. Beats all how nice it is here. Somethin' companionable in the smell of a hoss."

Misty, as if in appreciation, offered to shake hands.

"Sorry, gal. No time for tricks 'n treats today. Now then, Paul, come along. We can't keep the DUKW man waiting forever, and I got to see 'bout my herd up to Deep Hole."

116

Tom Reed was getting into his boat when the DUKW reached his place on the north end of the island. "Figured ye'd come along about now," he called. "Get out of that new-fangled contraption, Beebe, and climb aboard my old scow."

"How come she didn't get blowed away, same as mine?" Grandpa asked as he and Paul waded over. "And how come you and the missus didn't evacuate?"

"I tied her up to the rafters of my barn, that's why."

Paul grinned. "Is she still hanging there?"

Tom chuckled at the idea. "No, son, 'twas the boat. Truth is, Marjie just flat refused to go."

The driver of the DUKW was turning around, ready to leave. "Hey, Mr. Beebe," he shouted, "how soon should I come back?"

Tom answered for him. "No telling, captain. Could be all day. Ye'll just have to keep checking."

As Paul climbed into the boat, he noticed a bundle of sticks and a cellophane bag stuffed with pieces of cloth. "What they for, Tom?" he asked.

"They're rags from my wife's scrap bag. They're to make flags to mark where the dead animals are. Can't expect the 'copters to find 'em if they don't know where they be."

Although the air was bitter cold, the wind had lessened and holes of blue sky showed through the clouds. But the water about them was muddy-brown and full of drift. Grandpa reached for an oar.

"Wait a minute!" Tom said. "I got strict instructions from Marjie to give you coffee afore we set out. Wait a minute."

Grandpa guffawed. "We got a cat by that name 'cause she never does."

Paul broke in excitedly. "And she just had four kittens —Matthew, Mark, Luke, and John."

"Well, I'll be a chipmunk's tail," Grandpa chortled in surprise. "No worse'n namin' people for saints who they don't resemble a-tall."

"Easy to remember, too," Tom said, "and no hurt feelings if you call one by t'other." He was pouring thick black coffee into the lid of his thermos. "Its extry stout," he said, offering it first to Paul, "to fortify us for what's ahead."

Paul tasted it, trying not to make a face. Then he gulped it down, feeling it burn all the way.

Grandpa sipped his, meditating. "Over to Assateague," he thought aloud, "over in those dunes there's plenty hollows to ketch nice clean rain. Whatever ponies is left, there's places for 'em to drink. But here . . ." All at once he dumped the rest of his coffee overboard. "We got to rescue the live ones *right now,* or they'll bloat on this brackish water. Let's go!" he bellowed.

With Tom directing, they each took an oar and poled off into the morass. It was heavy going. The sludgy water was choked with boards from smashed chicken houses, and with briar and bramble and weedy vines so thickly interlaced it was like trying to break through a stout wire fence. Silently the three in the boat threaded their way along, stopping time and again to push rubbish aside and to scrape the seaweed from their oars.

Suddenly there came a thud and a jolt. The three oars lifted as one. All movement ceased. The men stared down in horror.

"Oh God!" Grandpa whispered. "It's my Black Warrior!"

118

No one spoke. Tom Reed reached down and took one colored square out of the bag and tied it to a stick. He drove the marker into the mud next to the stallion's body. " 'Twas a piece of Marjie's petticoat," he said nervously, just to say something. "I allus liked it with all the bright pink flowers."

Grandpa's eyes looked far off. "I was proud of the Warrior," he said quietly. "He used to help on Pony Penning Days to drive the really wild 'uns to the carnival grounds, and his tail was so long it swept the street, and his coat a-glistenin' like black sunshine. Recomember, Paul?" He wiped his arm across his eyes. Then his voice changed. "Move on!" he commanded. "We got to find the livin'."

The grim search went on. A quiet hung over the bog, except for the sloshing of oars and twigs snapping as the scow moved heavily along. Then a raucous, rasping sound sliced into the quiet of the morning.

"Look!" Paul cried. "Crows!"

The men poled faster until they came to a cloud of bold black birds flapping over a huddle of dead ponies.

Grandpa's face twisted in pain. "The Warrior's mares and colts," he said in utter desolation.

It was almost as if they were alive. Some were half-standing in the water, propped up by debris. They looked as if they were old and asleep.

"Guess they just died from exposure and cold." Tom's voice quavered, but his words were matter of fact. "One flag can do for all."

Grandpa got out of the boat and he grabbed the flag from Tom's hands. He stabbed it hard and fierce into the mud. Then he took a good look, and he began to name them all, saying a little piece of praise over each: "This one's a true Palomino. She had extry big ears, but gentle as the day, even though she'd never been rode. And this great big old tall mare was blind of one eye, but she had a colt ever' spring, reg'lar as dandylions. And this mare, she's got some pretty good age to her. She's somewhere in her twenty."

The crows came circling back, cawing at Grandpa. Angrily he whipped them away with his hat. "Likely she's had twelve, fifteen head in her day, and expectin' again." He sighed heavily. "That Black Warrior was a good stallion. He died tryin' to move his family to safety, but . . ." his voice broke ". . . they just couldn't move."

The heart-breaking work went on. They came upon snakes floating, and rabbits and rats. And they found more stallions dead, with their mares and colts nearby. And they found lone stragglers caught and tethered fast by twining vines. As the morning dragged into noon, and noon into cold afternoon, the pile of flags in the boat dwindled.

Sometimes an hour went by before they came on anything, alive or dead. Then Tom would chatter cheerfully, trying to lighten the burden. "Not ever'thing drowns," he said. "Early this morning I found me a snapper turtle under a patch of ice. He'd gone to sleep. Y'know, Paul, they snooze all winter, like bear."

Tom waited for an answer, but none came. "Funny thing about that little snapper," he went on, "he was a baby, no bigger'n a fifty-cent piece, and he was froze sure-enough. 'Tom,' I said to myself, 'he's dead.' But something tells me to put him in my inside pocket. And walking along I guess the heat of my body warmed him up, and guess what!"

120

"Grandpa!" Paul screamed. "I see something *alive!* In the woods!"

They turned the boat quickly and went poling through the soggy mass of kinksbush and myrtle. And there, caught among broken branches was a forlorn bunch of ponies, heads hanging low, their sides scarcely moving.

Grandpa slid overboard, trying not to make a splash,

trying not to panic them. Softly he called each one by name. "Nancy. Lucy. Polly. Gray Belle. Princess. Susy . . ."

The low, husky voice was like a lifeline thrown to drowning creatures. They lifted their heavy heads and one tried a whinny, but it was no more than a breath blowing. They were held fast, rooted in the boggy earth.

Tom and Paul were beside Grandpa in an instant. Without any signals between them, they knew what had to be done. They must drive the ponies to higher land near Tom's house, or they would die. Grim and determined, they maneuvered their way behind the ponies. Then grabbing pine boughs for clubs, they brandished them, whacking at the water, yelling like madmen, stirring the almost-dead things to life.

A pinto mare struggled free and led off in one desperate leap. The others stumbled after, trying to keep ahead of the wild thunder behind them. Scrabbling, crashing through uprooted trees, squeezing through bramble and thicket, they slogged forward inch by inch. And suddenly a mud-crusted stallion leaped out of the woods to join them.

"It's Wings!" Paul shrieked.

Men and ponies both were nearing exhaustion. But still they drove on. They *had* to. Shoving the boat, the men nosed it into the laggards, frightening them ever forward.

And at last they were in Tom's yard. Safe! As one, the ponies headed for the water barrel. Single-handed Grandpa overturned it, spilling out the dirty water tainted by the sea. He tried the spigot above it. "Pressure's good!" he exulted. "They got to blow first, then they can drink."

He and Tom and Paul were blowing too. But it was a healthy blow. *Something* at last had gone right.

Chapter 14

MISTY GOES TO POCOMOKE

IN THE HELICOPTER on the way back to Wallops Station, Grandpa and Paul talked things over. They would try to seal off today's grief. No need to speak of it tonight, with folks listening in. It would be like unbandaging a wound for everyone to see. They would talk of the kittens instead. And so, when the plane landed, their faces were set in a mask.

Maureen and Grandma, bundled in coats and scarves, were there to meet them. Maureen rushed up, bursting with curiosity. Before she could ask her question, Paul said, "You'd never, *ever* guess."

"All right, Mr. Smarty. Then I just won't try."

"There's more than one!"

"Twins?" she gasped. "Oh, Paul, isn't that wonderful! One for you and one for me!"

"Nope. It's quadruplets—it's four of them."

123

"Can't be!" Grandma broke in as they walked toward the mess hall. "I may be a sea-captain's daughter, but I know 'nough about ponies to know they don't have four to once. Speak up, Clarence."

Grandpa took off his hat and let the wind pick up the wisps of his hair. "Yup, Idy," he nodded, "yer kitchen's a nursery now with four little ones . . ."

Grandma wailed. "Oh, my beautiful new table all bit up, and my linoleum ruint."

"Pshaw! The little ones ain't bigger'n nothing," Grandpa said, flashing a wink at Paul.

At the door of the mess hall Maureen stopped in her tracks and began jumping up and down as if she had the answer to a riddle. "It's Wait-a-Minute!" she shouted. "She's had kittens again!"

Paul smiled. "Yep, Grandma's kitchen is a mew-seum now."

The children and even Grandma and Grandpa laughed in relief, not because they thought the joke so funny, but because it was good to be together again.

The refugee room had been transformed—cots lined up against the wall, neat as teeth in a comb, and new tables and chairs, and a television set with a half-circle of giggling children.

The Beebes went directly to their corner. Maureen and Grandma were still full of questions. But the answers were short.

"Yup, Misty's okay."

"No, no sign of Skipper anywheres."

"Rabbit's gone, too."

"Yup, our house is dry, 'cept for a tiny bit of wetting in one o' the bedrooms." Here Grandpa pinched his nose, remembering. "But it's got a odor to it that'll hold you."

In her dismay over her house, Grandma had forgotten all about Grandpa's ponies. Now as she helped him pull off his sweater, she asked, "What about your ninety head, Clarence? Are they . . ."

Paul kept very still, and Grandpa's old leathery face did not change expression. He looked dead ahead. "There was losses," was all he said. He turned to Maureen, and his voice was tight and toneless. "Me and Paul have done a lot of yelling today, and we're both wore out. We just don't feel talky, do we, Paul?"

"No, Grandpa."

"Suppose you and Grandma be like Red Cross angels and tote our suppers over here. We'd ruther not eat up to the big table with ever'body."

As Maureen and Grandma heaped the trays and carried them back, Maureen's lip quivered. "Oh, Grandma, Paul didn't even ask what I did today. He doesn't even know I was at Doctor Finney's, riding a famous trotter. Oh, Grandma, why was I born a girl?"

"It's God's plan, Maureen. Oops! Take care. Ye're spilling the soup."

Friday. The fourth day of the storm. Gray skies over Chincoteague. Rain off and on. Temperature rising. Wind and tide slowly subsiding. The causeway in use again—red ambulances carrying off the sick, yellow school buses the well, dump trucks removing the dead chickens.

Misty in the kitchen at Pony Ranch is growing restless. Her hay is gone. The water in the sink is gone. She is bored with the squeaky, squirmy kittens, and tired of looking out the window. Nothing seems to happen. No ponies frisking. No dog teasing her to come out and play. No birds flying. No friendly human creatures.

The room is getting too warm. Her winter coat itches. Even the bony part of her tail itches. She looks for something to scratch against. The handle of the refrigerator! She backs up to it. To her surprise the door kicks right back at her! She

wheels around, barely missing the mewing kittens. She pokes her head in the box, sniffing and nosing. She tries to fit her tongue into a pitcher of molasses. Crash! A dark dribble spills down on the kittens, on Wait-a-Minute too.

At last Misty has something to do. Good sweet molasses to clean up. She licks Wait-a-Minute, and Wait-a-Minute licks her kittens. The steady strokes bring on rumbly purring sounds. Misty grows drowsy. She turns to lie down, but the kittens are in her way. At last she sleeps, standing over them.

Afternoon came, and with it strange happenings. Paul and Grandpa arrived at Pony Ranch. This time their concern over Misty was desperate.

"A day or two at most," Grandpa said gravely.

"*You been saying that!*" Paul replied accusingly.

"I know." Grandpa looked crestfallen as if he'd failed in his duty. He made up his mind on the spot. "We're carryin' her over to Doc Finney's today, *to once!*"

They led Misty out of the house and into the old truck. They stowed a bundle of hay in its accustomed place, just as if she were going off to a school or a library story hour.

"You wait, Misty, we'll be right back," Grandpa said. "Paul and me got to give the kitchen a quick lick."

"Oh, do we *have* to?" Paul was all impatience.

"Yes, son. Some way I got a hunch yer Grandma's coming home right soon."

Back in the kitchen Paul and Grandpa mucked out the old straw, and gave the floor a hasty cleaning.

"Gives you a new regard for wimmenfolk, don't it, Paul?" Grandpa asked, dipping the broom into a pail of suds.

"Why?"

"Well, how'd *you* like to get down on yer knees and scrub suds and dirt together and try to get a slick surface?"

"I'd ruther muck out stalls."

"That's what I mean. Misty is what I'd call a tidy pony. She uses one corner and keeps ever'thing mounded up real neat. But even so—!"

When they had done the best they could, they turned to inspect their handiwork. The room looked better, they admitted, with the kittens in the laundry basket and the straw swept out and the molasses fairly well cleaned up, but somehow the pattern of the linoleum was gone.

"Oh, well," Grandpa sighed, "yer Grandma'll say, 'Clarence Beebe, this floor looks like a hurrah's nest.' And then she'll get right down with her brush and pail, and she'll begin purrin' and hummin' like Wait-a-Minute with her kittens. So let's leave it to her and get on with Misty."

Driving the truck through town to the causeway took an hour instead of minutes. The streets were filled with men

and machines. Huge bulldozers were pushing sand back into the bay and rubble into piles for burning.

Every time the truck had to stop, Misty was recognized and men shouted questions.

"Where ye taking Misty?"

"To Doctor Finney's!"

"Clear to Pocomoke City?"

"But why now, when the weather's fairin' off?"

" 'Cause she needs a doctor, that s why," Grandpa answered. "She's way past her time."

"Shucks, you never done this with your other ponies."

"But they're used to wild ways," Paul broke in. "Misty's more like folks."

"My grandchildren set a mighty store by her," Grandpa said. "We just can't chance it."

In front of his house the Mayor came out and flagged them down. "Beebe," he said, looking heavy-eyed and discouraged, "we're having a time getting those carcasses airlifted."

"How come?"

"The government has approved sending 'copters to take fresh water to the ponies still alive on Assateague, but they have no orders yet to take out the dead ones."

Grandpa exploded. "Mayor! The live ones has *got* water. There's allus water in the high-up pools in the White Hills. Them ponies know it."

"You and I know it too, Clarence. But sometimes outside people get sentimental in the wrong places. They mean well enough," he added with a tired smile. "It's the same old story about the evacuation. Even though the drinking water is piped to Chincoteague from the mainland, the Health Department still says no women or children can return yet."

Grandpa's face went red. "Mayor, I guess you don't need me to tell you the wimmenfolk is madder'n fire and sputterin' like wrens. Less'n they get home soon and tote their soggy mattresses and chairs out in the air, ever'thing'll be spoilt."

"Yes, I know. I know. I'm doing the best I can to get things cleared up. Right now I have a call in for our Senator in Washington. Perhaps he can get some action for us."

"But how about all the folk who didn't evacuate?"

"We can't force them to leave their homes, Clarence. But those that are at Wallops Station just can't come back until all the dead animals are removed. And Clarence," he called as Grandpa shifted into gear, "when the order does come through, we'll want you to help with the airlifting."

On the long trip to Pocomoke, Grandpa kept grumbling and muttering to himself.

Paul couldn't keep his eyes open. With Misty close by him, where he could reach back and touch her, he suddenly felt easy and relaxed, easier than he had since the storm began. He tried to stay awake. He tried to listen to Grandpa. He tried to watch the scenery. But his eyelids drooped. Finally he crawled in with Misty and slept on the floor beside her.

When at last they turned into Dr. Finney's place, Grandpa had to shake him awake.

Chapter 15

GRANDPA MAKES A DEAL

DR. FINNEY was a big man, outwardly calm, but his face looked as if it knew patience and pain.

"What do you think, sir?" Paul asked as they stood with Misty in the paddock.

"Well, to be frank, she's a little too heavy, Paul. That is, for one so fine-boned. And that's never good at a time like this. But we'll pull her through."

Misty shouldered her way into the center of the group, ears listening and questing, as if she were part of the conference instead of the cause.

The doctor put a gentle hand on Paul's shoulder. "Misty won't be lonesome here," he said. "In the next stall she can neighbor with Trineda, a well-bred trotter. And my boy

David can comfort her and take your place—for the time being," he added quickly.

Just then Dr. Finney's son came racing out of the house. Paul almost hated the boy on sight, for Misty trotted right up to him, sniffing curiously.

"Doctor Finney," Paul said urgently, "couldn't I stay here? Please?"

Grandpa answered before the doctor had finished clearing his throat. "If ye could be of help, me and Doc'd both say yes. But ye're needed over to Chincoteague. Lots o' moppin' up to be done, and ye volunteered as an able-bodied *man*. Recomember?"

Still Paul could not bring himself to go. He slid his hand under Misty's mane, scruffing his fingers along. "Doctor Finney," he asked, "would it be a good idea for us to get a nanny goat just in case . . . ?"

The doctor was about to say it wouldn't be necessary. Then he saw the troubled look on the boy's face. Better, he thought, to keep him busy instead of worrying. "It wouldn't hurt at all, Paul. Many breeding stables keep a goat for that very purpose. By the way," he turned now to Grandpa, "you must know Buck Jackson from Chincoteague."

Grandpa flinched. "Yup, I know him. Sells goat's milk."

"Well, he's delivering a flock of goats to Girdletree today, and I'm to give them a health certificate. If you'd like to buy a nanny, I'll ask Buck if he can spare one. But you'd have to keep her at Pony Ranch, because I'm short of space."

Grandpa shrugged helplessly. "Allus it's me against the world," he said, half joking, half in earnest. Then he stared down the highway in amazement.

132

A shining white truck was barreling along toward them. Now it was slowing, and in big black letters on its side Grandpa made out the words:

BUCK JACKSON DELIVERY—GOAT'S MILK.

With a screeching of tires the truck turned into the driveway and came to a stop. A big-shouldered man jumped down from the cab and opened the tailgate. "Hi, Paul and David," he called. "Hi, Doc. Hi, Mr. Beebe. Hi, Misty. Heavens-to-Betsy, I didn't expect a welcoming committee!"

Misty and Paul and David were first to peer inside. The two boys were suddenly friends, buyers, judging an odd assortment of goats.

Grandpa stuck his nose into the truck and sniffed noisily. "I jes' don't like 'em," he insisted. "They smell from here to Kingdom Come. To me, a polecat smells purtier."

But Paul was ecstatic. "They can't help it, Grandpa.

And besides, Misty needs someone to play with, now that Skipper's gone."

"She'll have her colt," Grandpa reminded.

Paul was not listening. "I like that brown nanny with the little white kid."

"So do I," David agreed. "And if I was your Grandpa, I'd let you have the whole truckload," he offered generously.

"Who says I want to sell any?" Buck Jackson asked.

That did it. Grandpa was a born trader. "Buck," he said, "there's lots o' goats over to Chincoteague. Some nicer'n yours. Cy Eustace has a hull flock, and Ben Sykes has . . ."

"Not any more they don't. They're drowned."

Grandpa ignored the interruption. "But since my grandson has took a fancy to that brown one and her kid, what'll ye take for the pair?"

Buck winked at Dr. Finney. "I'll take Misty and her unborn."

Now Grandpa's blood was up. "Quit yer jokin'!"

"Who says I'm jokin'?"

In the waiting silence Misty poked her head inside the truck and the brown goat gave her a friendly butt. Misty came right back, asking for more.

"I give up!" Grandpa sighed. He pulled out his ancient leather purse and began fumbling inside, transferring bits of string and wire to a pocket. At last he held out a much-folded five-dollar bill. "This may seem mighty little to ye, but hoss-keepin' ain't what ye'd call profitable. Here, take it."

Buck Jackson chewed on a toothpick, thinking. "If I didn't say yes," he said at last, "even Misty here'd hate me. It's a deal, Clarence, and I'll throw in a bale of hay besides."

The transaction was quickly completed. But even
the nanny and her kid in the pickup, Paul didn't find it eas.
to say good-bye to Misty. "Don't ride her," he cautioned
David. "She's going to have a colt."

"I know she is," David replied in disgust. "*Everybody* knows that."

Dr. Finney held onto Misty's halter. "Don't you worry, Paul. I'll sleep in the stall next to her, and I'll stay within sight and sound during her foaling period."

"You promise?"

"I promise."

It was almost dark when Grandpa and Paul crossed the state line back into Virginia.

"Tradin' whets my appetite," Grandpa confided to Paul. "What d'ye say we stop by Wallops Station and have some nice hot Red Cross food with Grandma and Maureen?"

"What about our goats? Shouldn't we hurry home and put them in the hay house with Billy Blaze and Watch Eyes? They got to get used to being with horses."

Grandpa wasn't listening. A flicker of a smile crossed his face. "Don't interrupt me, son. My mind's turnin' over important thoughts."

The refugee room looked much the same, except for more cots and more people. And it still smelled of old rubber and leather and steamy woolen socks.

As the family sat down at the long table, Paul whispered to Maureen, "I like the smell of goats better'n people, and we got two—a nanny and a kid."

"Oh, Paul, how beautiful!"

"They're not beautiful; they're really kind of funny-looking with their eyes so different from horses'."

"I know. They're bluey-yellow, and they look glassy, like marbles."

136

Paul and Maureen could hardly eat for all they had to say to each other.

"Misty's at Doctor Finney's, Maureen. She can't keep on postponing forever and she can't go on living in Grandma's kitchen. Ain't healthy and airy for her. And besides . . ."

"Besides what?"

"I overheard the doctor say there could be complications."

Grandma and Grandpa were deep in conversation, too. Grandpa seemed to have forgotten he was hungry. "Idy," he said, "Pony Ranch is now the owners of a nanny goat and her kid. A billy-kid, at that! It's got whiskers as long as yer sea-captain pa."

"Clarence Beebe! Don't you talk like that. I'll not have ye comparin' my father to a billy goat!"

"Oh, come now, Idy. I'm jes' bein' jokey. Besides, yer father smelled real good—of tobaccy and things. By the way," he asked, trying to appear casual, "you and Maureen had yer arms scratched against the typhoid?"

Grandma nodded.

"Good! I'm turribly glad."

"Why? Is the typhoid raging?"

"No, but I need ye at home, Idy, to perten me up for what I got to do."

"What's that?" Grandma asked in alarm.

"I got to see that all my dead ponies is taken off'n Chincoteague, and the dead ones on Assateague, too."

"Oh . . . oh, how dreadful! But they say wimmenfolk can't go home now. Regardless."

"I know they *say* so." Grandpa's eyes crinkled with his secret. "But *I* say the Lord helps them as helps theirselves."

Grandma looked at him questioningly.

"Idy, how'd ye like to . . . ?"

"Like to what?"

Grandpa sopped up some tomato gravy with a chunk of bread and ate it slowly, enjoying Grandma's impatience. Then he leaned close to her ear. "How'd ye and Maureen like to be smuggled back home? Right now!"

Grandma beamed. "Be ye serious?"

"Serious as a cow at milkin' time."

"Why, mercy me, I'd feel young and chipper doin' a thing like that."

"Ye would?"

"Yes, I would."

"Even if ye had to hide in the back o' a truck under a bundle o' hay with goats eatin' through to ye?"

"Even if!" Grandma hurriedly left the table, motioning Maureen and Paul to follow. "Don't ask any questions," she said. "Just slip into your jackets and come along, and leave our blankets on the cots."

The people nearby looked up in surprise as the Beebe family put on their wraps.

"My husband has got some goats down in the truck he wants us to see," Grandma explained.

"But it's raining, Mrs. Beebe."

"I know. That's why we're bundling up." Grandma blushed. "Y'see, my husband's like a little boy whenever he's got a new pet to show me."

Chapter 16

WELCOME HOME, PROGGER

THE NIGHT was dark and broody with no moon or stars. Not a glimmer of light anywhere. A curtain of fine rain closed in the deserted parking lot.

With a great heave Grandpa hoisted Grandma up into the back of the truck. "It's easier loading Misty," he panted.

Grandma was too excited to answer. Feeling her way in the dark, she pushed the goats aside, took off her head scarf, and sat down on it. Then she opened a clean handkerchief for Maureen. But Maureen ignored it, lost in delight over the little white kid.

The motor made a roar in the night as the truck pulled out of the lot and headed for the highway. Almost there, Grandpa turned down a gravel lane, dimmed the lights, and parked. He and Paul jumped out and ran to the back of the truck. Hastily they broke open the bale of hay, and began shaking it over the stowaways.

Maureen sneezed.

"Hay's dusty," Paul said.

"Might of knowed it," Grandpa snorted. "No wonder Buck Jackson give it away. Now whichever of ye sneezed, we can't have no more o' that. If yer nose feels tickly, jes' clamp yer finger hard underneath it, and 'twon't happen."

Before Paul and Grandpa got back into the cab, they looked around cautiously. No one was in sight.

"I feel like the smugglers we read about in Berlin," Paul said, "sneakin' refugees to West Germany."

It was only a half-hour's ride to Chincoteague, but with no one singing or laughing, it seemed more like half a day. In silence they rode past Rabbit Gnaw Road and through Horntown and past Swan's Gut Road and across the salt flats that led to the causeway.

Almost at the end of the causeway their headlights showed up a temporary guardhouse. A soldier with a rifle came out and flagged them down. He shone his flashlight into the cab of the truck. "Hi there, Mr. Beebe," he grinned in recognition. "Hi, Paul. How's Misty?"

"She's still all right," Paul replied.

The guard flicked off his flashlight and leaned one arm on the lowered window. He seemed hungry for talk. "Funny thing," he said, "about the telephone calls comin' in from all over the countryside. Mostly they're from children. It's not folks they're worried about. It's the ponies. 'Specially Misty. Yeah," he laughed, "*she's* their prime concern."

"Mine, too!" Paul said.

Unmindful of the drizzle, the guard went on. "By the way, how's everybody over at Wallops?"

Grandpa coughed. "They're all hankerin' fer home."

"Wal, maybe it won't be long now. The Mayor got through to Washington, and they're sending four big 'copters tomorrow to work with you and Tom on liftin' the dead ponies." In a routine manner he went around to the back of the truck and flashed his light inside. "Any stowaways?" he asked jokingly.

Grandpa matched the joking tone. "Yup, we got two."

After an interminable silence the soldier's laughter filled the night. "Wal, I'll be a billy goat's whiskers if ye 'ain't got a nanny and her kid! How's the missus going to like that?"

"I figger she's going to feel mighty close to 'em," Grandpa chuckled.

"Why? How's that?"

Suddenly Grandpa panicked. The sweat came cold on his forehead. He cut off the dashlight so his face would be in the dark. He couldn't speak.

Paul came to the rescue. "We bought them for Misty's colt," he explained. "Sup-pli-ament-ary feeding, you know."

The guard snapped off his light and tweaked Paul's ear. "Ye got a bright boy here, Mr. Beebe. G'night, folks. Ye can move on now."

Home was clammy cold, and it had a stench of fish, and the bedroom rug with the roses was wet as a sponge. But it was Home! And Wait-a-Minute was there with a wild welcome, turning somersaults, then flying round and round like a whirling dervish.

"This floor is like walkin' on mucilage," Grandma said, "but no matter how messy, there's jes' no place like Pony Ranch."

Maureen sighed in agreement. Then she added soberly, "Even without the ponies."

"You forget," Paul corrected, "we still have Watch Eyes and Billy Blaze, and the mares in the hay house."

"And," Grandpa added with a crooked smile, "Wings' herd up to Tom's Place . . . and with Misty expectin' . . . and two goats and five cats, we got the beginnin's again."

"Grandma!" Maureen cried. "What's happened to the back of your dress?"

Grandma swished her skirt around. Her eyes widened. The whole back from the waist down was gone. "Why, whatever in the world!" she gasped.

Paul and Maureen began to shriek in laughter. "The nanny goat!"

"Like I said," Grandpa roared, "Missus Beebe'll allus feel mighty close to that nanny."

Grandma flounced to the drawer where she kept her aprons. In pretended anger she took out two. "I'll just wear 'em both," she said. "One fore and one aft."

There was much to be done before bedtime—the ponies in the hay house to be grained and watered, the nanny and her kid to be tended to, kindling to be brought in. And late as it was, Grandma got down on her hands and knees and scrubbed the floor with vigor and strong naphtha soap.

When she had almost finished, Maureen, muddy but radiant, sloshed into the back hall. "Guess what, Grandma!"

"What *now?*" Grandma asked without looking up. Her lips were set in a thin line as she carefully pushed the basket of kittens back under the stove. "Now what you so tickled about?"

"Feel in my pocket!"

"Mice?"

"No, Grandma. Guess again."

"Probably some toady-frog or lizard."

"No! No! Feel!"

Grandma wiped her hands on her apron and poked a cautious fingertip into Maureen's pocket. She touched something smooth and curved. Smiling, she reached in and brought out two tiny brown-flecked eggs.

"And there's two in my other pocket! I found 'em high and dry in Misty's manger."

Grandpa and Paul came stomping into the back hall with armfuls of wood. "What's to eat?" Grandpa shouted. "I could swaller a whale."

Grandma shook her head. "Bread's mouldy. Milk's sour. Only thing we got is four little bitty banty eggs."

"Why, they're good," Maureen said in a hurt tone.

" 'Course they are, honey." Grandma placed them on the table. "Paul, you still got your boots on. Run out to the smoke-house for some bacon. We'll have a tiny fried egg apiece and plenty o' crispy bacon. I'll put the skillet on and have it spittin' hot."

When Paul had gone out, Grandma turned to Maureen and Grandpa. "Now you two wash up so's I can tell who's who. And for pity's sake, use that naphtha soap. If'n I had any sense at all, I'd go around this house with a clothespin twigged onto my nose."

Grandpa's face broadened into a grin. "Humpf! A sea-captain's daughter complainin' 'bout a little bilge water."

Suddenly Maureen shushed Grandpa and held up a warning finger. "Listen!"

Faint and far off, like something in a dream, came a sound like a dog's barking. Then it faded away and stopped. They all stood still—waiting, listening. For long seconds they heard nothing. Only the clock hammering and the fire crackling in the stove.

But there! It came again. Louder this time. Nearer! A gruff, rusty bark, then three short yaps, familiar, beloved.

In one stride Grandpa was at the door. He flung it wide

and a flash of golden fur bulleted into the room, skidding across the wet floor until it reached Maureen.

"Skipper! Skipper!" she cried, hugging him passionately, wildly.

Grandpa and Grandma seemed to forget they were grown. They let Skipper come leaping at them, let him put his front feet on their shoulders. Who minded muddy paws? Who minded the icy-cold nose? Who minded the wet tongue-swipes? And the tracked floor? Not even Grandma! Only Wait-a-Minute hissed and spat at him.

Everyone was laughing and crying and talking all at once.

"Where you been, feller?"

"*I* thought you'd been caught in a mushrat trap."

"*I* thought you'd drowned, for sure."

"Why, ye're strong as a tiger."

"And yer coat's got a nice shine."

Paul came in then, a wide smile spread across his face. "He *should* be fat and shiny. He's been in the smokehouse eatin' his way through hams and salt pork."

Grandma wiped her laughter-tears away. "He allus was crazy on smoked meats," she said.

Maureen buried her nose in his ruff. "He's even got a smokehouse smell to him," she said. "Remember, Paul? Last thing you did was to go get a ham before we left on the helicopter."

Grandpa went to the sink and plunged his face into the wash basin, making a sound like a seal. He came up bellowing: "Skipper's a progger!"

"What's that?" Maureen and Paul wanted to know.

Grandpa scruffed his beard, thinking. "It's a old, old Chincoteague word, and it means . . . wa–al, it jes' means someone as is smart enough to grab a livin' when things is dire bad." And he cupped his hands around his mouth and boomed, "Welcome home, ye old Progger!"

146

Chapter 17

SAWDUST AND SADNESS

SATURDAY. News briefs from around the world were coming over the radio like flak:

"India agrees to a conference with Pakistan. . . . African leaders at the United Nations are exploring the Common Market. . . . Russia accuses the United States of warmongering. . . . Jordan and Israel again at loggerheads over the River Jordan. . . . England's Queen Elizabeth and Prince Philip return in triumph from Australia and New Zealand."

The newscaster paused and took a breath as if all this were far away and only a prelude to the real news. His tone became neighborly now and concerned.

"And here on the home front, the tiny flooded island of Chincoteague has aroused the sympathy of the whole nation. The islanders, whose livelihood depends on chickens and seafood and ponies, have suffered a savage blow to all three industries. Their oyster beds are gone; their chickens are gone. And today's report indicates that only a remnant of the wild pony herds on Assateague Island have survived. These are the ponies that made Chincoteague famous for the annual round-up and Pony Penning celebration, and that have brought visitors by the thousands. How seriously this loss will affect the tourist industry can only be estimated.

"Yet the Chincoteaguers are showing indomitable courage. With bulldozers and scoop shovels they are pushing tons of sand off streets, off lawns, out of cellars, and back into the channel. Clean-up crews are making bonfires of rubble and debris.

"Oh . . . flash news! Two notes were just handed me. One says Misty, the movie-star pony, has been evacuated from her owner's kitchen to an animal hospital in Pocomoke, Maryland, where her colt is expected momentarily.

"The other says the Second Army at Fort Belvoir is flying in helicopters within the hour to remove the dead ponies from Chincoteague and Assateague . . ."

At Pony Ranch Grandpa snapped off the radio in mid-sentence. "I got to go now," he said in a tone of finality. "Them's my orders." He kissed his family good-bye as solemnly as if he were going away on a long journey and might never return.

"No, son." He shook his head in answer to Paul's asking look. "No, ye're needed here today to work on Misty's stall.

Somebody's got to ready it for her homecoming. Besides, Grandma and Maureen can't lift that wet rug out on the line by theirselves. They need an able-bodied man."

"But who's going to help lift the dead po—"

Grandpa cut off the word with a sharp glance. His eyes said, "Less talk, the better." And his voice said, "Each 'copter has a crew of four stout army men, and there's Tom Reed and Henry Leonard to help me."

Grandma's eyes were bright with unshed tears. Quickly she went to the cupboard and took out a small brown sack. "I was saving these peppermints for Misty's baby. But here, Clarence, you take them. For extry strength," she whispered, "when things is rough."

Paul and Maureen were soon so busy with preparations for Misty's return that they forgot Grandpa. The phone might ring any minute, long distance, with big news from Pocomoke. And if it did, the made-over chicken coop had to be dry and snug and warm, and waiting.

The day was spent in a fever of activity. At first they tackled the heavy, sodden straw with enthusiasm. They were used to cleaning Misty's stall every morning before breakfast. It took only a few minutes—fifteen at most. But now clumps of seaweed made the bedding slithery as soup and heavy as lead. With fork and shovel they pitched and tossed for an hour. Each wheelbarrowful seemed heavier than the last, until finally it took both of them, one at each handle, to push it and dump the muck in the woods.

Skipper found an old pulpy potato and asked Paul and Maureen to play ball, but they were too busy and too tired.

At morning's end the floor of the shed was emptied of wet bedding, but what remained was a churned-up, slimy mass of mud. Maureen leaned against the wall, rubbing an arm across her face. "How are we *ever* going to get it dry?" she said, bursting into tears.

Paul felt defeated too, and his head and body ached. "What we need," he groaned, "is a thousand million blotters. But where?" Suddenly his face lighted in inspiration. "Sawdust!" he cried. "That's what we need!" He ran sloshing toward the road, calling back over his shoulder, "You wait, I'm going to see Mr. Hancock."

Mr. Hancock was a long-time friend. He was a wood-carver, and had given work to Paul and Maureen when they were earning money to buy Misty's mother. Often for fifty cents apiece they had swept his shop clean of sawdust and shavings.

By the time Maureen had finished her cry and wiped away her tears, Paul and Mr. Hancock were driving into the yard in his newly painted truck. She gaped in astonishment as she watched them unload bushel basket after bushel basket of sawdust at the door of the stall.

"Ain't near enough," Mr. Hancock said as he helped dump the yellow sawdust on the floor and saw it turn dark and wet in seconds. "Tell ye what," he said, noticing Maureen's tear-streaked face, "it's eatin'-time now and we all got to eat, regardless. That'll give this stuff time to absorb all the wet it's a-goin' to. Then ye got to heave it all out, and I'll bring more sawdust, and some chips too. Lucky thing I had it stored high and dry in my barn loft."

Paul piled the empty baskets into Mr. Hancock's truck.

151

Then he and Maureen headed wearily for the house. Maureen was trying not to cry.

"See what I see?" Paul pointed to the back stoop. And there was Grandma milking the nanny goat, who was tied to the stair railing.

"Sh . . . sh!" Grandma warned as the children came up. "Don't frighten her. This ain't easy, but I got eenamost enough to make us a nice pot of cocoa."

All during lunch Grandma kept up a stream of conversation to cheer them. "Children," she said brightly, "a she-goat was 'zackly what we needed. If not for Misty, then for us. Ain't this cocoa *de*-licious?"

Paul and Maureen nodded, too tired for words.

"You can each have two cups. And all the biscuits you can eat, with gooseberry jam. I figger the starving people of the world would think this a Thanksgiving feast, don't ye?"

"Yes, Grandma."

"And since you still got work on Misty's stall, you don't need to hang my rug outside today. I got all the windows open and there's a good breeze blowing in."

"Thank you, Grandma."

"Now, you two perten up. Everything's going to be better this afternoon. Life's like a teeter-totter. Heartbreak, happiness. Happiness, heartbreak. You'll see. Everything'll be better this afternoon."

Grandma was right. By the time the wet sawdust was shoveled out, Mr. Hancock was back again with a small tow wagon hooked onto his car.

"Got a big surprise fer ye," he chuckled. "The road people was putting down some ground-up oyster shells, and I got 'em to fill my wagon plumb full. With them shells first, and the shavings atop that, ye'll have the driest stable this side o' Doc Finney's."

The rest of the afternoon flew by in a fury of work. Paul dumped the oyster shells onto the floor. Maureen raked them even. Then came layer on layer of chips and shavings. For a final touch they took a bale of straw and cut it up, a sheaf at a time, into short wisps.

"Why can't we just shake it airy?" Maureen asked. "My fingers ache. Why do I have to cut it?"

"Do you want his pipestem legs getting all tangled up and throwin' him down?"

" 'Course not. When you tell me why, I don't mind doing it. But, Paul, how do you know it's going to be a 'he'?"

"I don't, silly. People always say 'he' when they don't know."

"Well, *I* say 'she.' "

With the work done, Paul flopped down on the straw and lay there quite still.

"You sick?" Maureen asked in fright.

"No!"

"Then what are you doing?"

"I'm a newborn colt and I'm testing to see if there are any draughts. Doctor Finney says they can't stand them."

"I feel the wind coming in through the siding. I can feel it blowing my hair."

"That's easy to fix." Paul got up and plastered the cracks with straw and mud. Meanwhile Maureen stripped some pine branches and scattered the needles lightly for fragrance.

By twilight any horse-master would have tacked a blue ribbon on the old chicken-coop barn. Maureen called Grandma to come out and inspect. "You've got to see, Grandma. It's beautiful. Misty's going to be the happiest mother in the world."

Grandma, holding her sweater tight around her neck, stepped inside the snug shelter. She beamed her approval. "I declare to goodness, I'd like to move in myself. Just wait 'til yer Grandpa sees this. Likely he'll do a hop-dance for joy."

But that night Grandpa never even looked at Misty's stall. It was dark when he came home. Without a word he made his way toward the kitchen table and sat down heavily. His face seemed made of clay, gray and pinched and old. Without removing his jacket he sat there, hands folded, just staring at the floor.

The noisy clock was no respecter of grief. Each stroke of the hammer thudded like a heartbeat. The seconds and minutes ticked on. Paul and Maureen sat very still, saying nothing, doing nothing. Just waiting.

"Yer Grandpa's had a mill day," Grandma whispered at last. "He's all cut to pieces. Jes' leave him be."

It was as if the gentle words had broken a dike. The old man hid his face in his arms and wept.

"Don't be ashamed to cry, Clarence. Let the tears out if they want to come." Grandma put her clean, scrubbed hand on the gnarled, mud-crusted ones. "King David in the Bible was a strong man and he wept copiously." Her voice went on softly. "In my Sunday School class just two weeks ago I gave the story of King David. There was one verse and it said, 'The King covered his face and wept.' Just like you, Clarence."

Neither Paul nor Maureen made a sound. They were too stunned. They watched the heaving shoulders in silence. Grandpa, who had always seemed so strong and indestructible, now looked little and feeble and old. When his sobs quieted, he wiped his eyes and slowly looked up. "I ain't fit to talk to nobody," he said, his voice no more than a breath.

"Oh . . . oh, Grandpa!" Maureen cried. "Your voice! It's gone! You ain't bellerin'!" And she ran to him and flung her arms about him, sobbing hysterically.

155

"There, there, child. Don't you cry, too. I'm plumb 'shamed to break down when we're lots luckier than most folks." He smiled weakly. "We got our house and each other and . . . "

"And Misty," Paul said earnestly.

"And Misty," Grandpa nodded. "It's jes'. . . ." He swallowed hard and his hands gripped the table until the knuckles showed white through the dirt. "It's jes'," he repeated, "that all the days of my life I'll hear that slow creakin' of the crane liftin' up the dead ponies, and I'll see their legs a-swingin' this way and that like they was still alive and kickin'." Now the words poured from him in a tide; he couldn't stop the flow. "And some had stars on their faces, and some had two-toned manes and tails, and some was marked so bright and purty, and most o' the mares had a little one inside 'em." His voice broke. "I knowed all my herd by name."

"How many were there in all, Clarence? Yours and the others?"

Grandpa's breath came heavy, as if he were still at work. "We lifted off more'n we could count," he said, "includin' the wild ones over to Assateague. And when the trucks was all lined up with their dead cargo, ever' one of us took off our hats, and the army men and us Chincoteaguers all looked alike with our sunburnt faces and white foreheads. And we was all alike in our sadness.

"Then the preacher, he come by and he said somethin' about these hosses needin' no headstone to mark their grave, and he put up a prayer to the memory of the wild free things. He said, 'Neither tide nor wind nor rain nor flight of time can erase the glory o' their memory.' "

156

Everyone in the little kitchen let out a deep sigh as if the preacher's words were right and good.

After a moment Grandpa got up from the table and put his arm around Grandma. "Now ye see, Idy, why I had to smuggle ye home. I needed ye for comfort."

Grandma wiped her spectacles with her apron. "Must be steam in the room," she said.

Grandpa had one more thing to say. "Fer jes' this oncet in my life I wisht I was a waterman 'stead of a hossman. When oysters die, ye can plant another bushel, and when boats drift away, ye can build another. But when ponies die . . . how can ye replace 'em?"

Paul glanced around in sudden terror. It was as if a cold blade of fear had struck him. His eyes sought Maureen's. They were very dark and wide and asking.

Was Misty all right?

Chapter 18

WITHIN THE FOALING BOX

ON THE same day that Grandpa was airlifting the ponies and Paul and Maureen were drying out Misty's stall, Misty herself felt strangely unhappy.

She had a freshly made bed in a snug stable, and she couldn't have been lonely for she was never without company. If she so much as scratched an ear with a hind hoof, young David Finney tried to do it for her. If she lipped at her hay, he tore handfuls out of the manger and presented it joyously to her. If she lay down, he tried to help her get comfortable.

And there were newspaper men coming and going, taking pictures of her in her stall, out of her stall, with David, without David. One caught Misty pulling the ponytail of a lady reporter. There was plenty of laughter and a constant flow of visitors.

But in spite of all the attention she was getting, Misty felt discontented and homesick. She was accustomed to the cries of sea birds, and the tang of salt air, and the tidal rhythm of the sea. And she was accustomed to going in and out of her stall, to the old tin bathtub that was her watering trough. But here everything was brought to her.

She kept shaking her head nervously and stamping in impatience. Occasionally she let out a low cry of distress which brought David and Dr. Finney on the run. But they could not comfort her. She yawned right in their faces as much as to say, "Go away. I miss my own home-place and my own children and my own marsh grass."

In all the long day there was only one creature who seemed to sense her plight. It was Trineda, the trotter in the next stall. The two mares struck up a friendly attachment, and when they weren't interrupted by callers, they did a lot of neighborly visiting. If Misty paced back and forth, Trineda paced alongside in her own stall, making soothing, snorting sounds. The newsmen spoke of her as Misty's lady-in-waiting, and some took pictures of the two, nose to nose.

When night came on, Trineda was put out to pasture, and Misty's sudden loneness was almost beyond bearing. She shied at eerie shadows hulking across her stall. And her ear caught spooky rustling sounds. Filled with uneasiness, she began pacing again, not knowing that the shadows came from a lantern flame flickering as the wind stirred it, not knowing that the rustling sounds were made by Dr. Finney tiptoeing

159

into the next stall, carefully setting down his bag of instruments, and stealthily opening up his sleeping roll.

When at last there was quiet, Misty lay down, trying to
get comfortable. But she was even more uncomfortable.
Hastily she got up and tried to sleep standing, shifting her
weight from one foot to another.

Suddenly she wanted to get out, to be free, to high-tail
it for home. She neighed in desperation. She pawed and
scraped the floor, then banged her hoof against the door.

Trineda came flying in at once, whinnying her concern. Trying to help, she worked on the catch to the door, but it was padlocked. She thrust her head inside, reaching over Misty's shoulder, as much as to say, "There, there. There, there. It'll all be over soon."

Dr. Finney watched, fascinated, as the four-footed nurse quickly calmed her patient. "It'll probably be a long time yet," he told himself. "Nine chances out of ten she'll foal in the dark watches of the night. I'd better get some sleep while I can." He was aware that many of his friends would pity him tonight, shaking their heads over the hard life of a veterinarian. But at this moment he would not trade jobs for any other in the world. Each birth was a different kind of miracle.

Sighing in satisfaction, he slid down into his sleeping bag and settled himself for a long wait. The seconds wore on, and the minutes and the slow hours. He grew drowsy and he dozed, and he woke to check on Misty, and he dozed again. Toward morning his sleep was fitful and he dreamed that Misty was a tree with ripening fruit—just one golden pear. And he dreamed that the stem of the fruit was growing weak, and it was the moment of ripe perfection.

A flush of light in the northeast brought him sharply awake. He peered through the siding and he saw Misty lying down, and he saw wee forehoofs breaking through the silken birth bag, the head resting upon them; then quickly came the slender body with the hindlegs tucked under.

He froze in wonder at the tiny filly lying there, complete and whole in the straw. It gave one gulping gasp for air, and then its sides began rising and falling as regularly as the ticking of a clock.

Alarmed by the gasping sound, Misty scrambled to her feet and turned to look at the new little creature, and the cord joining them broke apart, like the pear from the tree. Motionless, she watched the spidery legs thrashing about in the straw. Her foal was struggling to get up. And then it was half way up, nearly standing!

Suddenly Misty was all motherliness. She sniffed at the shivering wet thing and some warning impulse told her to protect it from chills. Timidly at first, she began to mop it dry with her tongue. Then as her confidence grew, she scrubbed in great rhythmic swipes. Lick! Lick! Lick! More vigorously all the time. The moments stretched out, and still the cleaning and currying went on.

Dr. Finney sighed in relief. Now the miracle was complete—Misty had accepted her foal. He stepped over the unneeded bag of instruments and picked up a box of salt and a towel. Then, talking softly all the while, he unlocked Misty's door and went inside. "Good girl, Misty. Move over. There, now. You had an easy time."

With a practiced hand he sprinkled salt on the filly's coat and the licking began all over again. "That's right, Misty. You work on your baby," he said, unfolding the towel, "and I'll rub *you* down. Then I'll make you a nice warm gruel. Why, you're not even sweating, but we can't take any chances."

Misty scarcely felt Dr. Finney's hands. She was nudging the foal with her nose, urging it up again so that she could scrub the other side.

The little creature *wanted* to stand. Desperately it thrust its forelegs forward. They skidded, then splayed into an

inverted V, like a schoolboy's compass. There! It was standing, swaying to and fro as if caught in a wind.

Smiling, Dr. Finney stopped his rubbing. He saw that all was well. Reluctantly he left the stall.

Minutes later he was on the telephone. Young David stood behind him, listening in amazement and disgust. How could grownups be so calm, as if they'd just come in from repairing a fence or pulling weeds? He wanted to do handsprings, cartwheels, stand on his head! But there was his father's voice again, sounding plain and everyday.

"Yes, Paul. She delivered at dawn."

"A mare colt, sound as a dollar."

"Yes, I'm making Misty a warm mash. Just waiting for it to cool a bit."

"No, Paul, she's just fine. Everything was normal."

"No, don't bring the nanny goat. Misty's a fine mother."

"Don't see why not. By mid-afternoon, anyway."

Dr. Finney put the receiver in place, stretching and yawning.

"Dad, what don't you 'see why not'?" David asked.

"Why they can't take Misty and her foal home today."

"Can I go out and see her now?" David pleaded.

"No, son," Dr. Finney replied. Then he saw the flushed young face and the tears brimming. "Of course you can go later. Just give them an hour or so alone."

Chapter 19

GLORY HALLELUJAH!

PAUL TURNED from the telephone and let out a war whoop loud enough to break the sound barrier. He grabbed Maureen and they pulled Grandpa between them and went dancing around the kitchen table, lifting their knees high, bugling like wild horses. It was a free-for-all frolic. Grandpa was suddenly himself again, spry-legged and bellowing.

Grandma laughed in relief. She dropped her spoon in the pancake batter and half ran to the organ. Recklessly she threw back the lid and, with all stops open, made the notes thunder and throb as she sang in her full-bodied voice:

165

"Glory, glory, halle-*loooo*-jah,
Glory, glory, halle-*loooo*-jah,
Glory, glory, halle-*loooo*-jah,
His truth is marching on."

Around and around the table marched the three Beebes.
Skipper burst into the house, joining the dance, howling to

the music. At last Grandpa had to sit down, and Paul and Maureen fell limp and exhausted on the floor.

Grandma turned from the organ, her eyes crinkled with joy. She clapped her hands for attention, then chanted:

> "*Come* day, *go* day;
> God send *Sun*-day.

And where do we go today?" she asked.

"To Pocomoke!" Maureen burst out.

"But before that, where? And who do we thank today?"

"Misty!" Paul shouted. But he grinned as he said it, knowing what Grandma had in mind.

Grandpa twisted uncomfortably. "Me and him," he said, scratching Skipper behind an ear, "we got to clean out the truck and do a passel o' things. We'll jes' do our churchin' while we work."

"Clarence Beebe, you'll do no sech a thing! Today is a shining special day and we won't argify. To church we go. *As a fambly!*"

Promptly at nine forty-five the truck, now clean as water and soap could make it, rattled out of the yard with Grandpa and Grandma sitting dressed up and proud in the cab, and Maureen and Paul in back, feet dangling over the tailgate. The sun was shining for the first time in a week, and the sky was a luminous blue.

"Seems almost like it's Easter," Maureen said. "Seems different from other Sundays. Wonder why?"

" 'Cause we're wearing shadow rolls over our noses, just like race horses."

Unconsciously Maureen felt of her nose.

"Can't you see, Maureen? We're not even looking at the houses with their porches ripped off and mattresses and things drying in the sun. We're seeing bigger."

"Like what?"

Paul looked up. "Like that flag flying over the Fire House, painting stars and stripes on the sky. And the sea smiling and cheerful as if it'd never been nasty-mean."

Maureen nodded. "And even if the houses *are* all bashed in, Paul, you hardly notice them for the clumps of daffydils."

It was true. The world seemed reborn. The blue-green water of the bay was unruffled and washing softly against the drift. Gulls were gliding on a seaward breeze with scarcely a wing-flutter. And here and there in all the mud and muck, hosts of yellow daffodils were nodding like spatters of sunshine.

Up in front Grandpa and Grandma were feeling the same joy. "The storm sure bloomed the place up," Grandpa said.

Grandma sighed in deep contentment. "Takes a wrathful storm to make us 'preciate bonny weather, don't it?"

As the Beebe family took their seats in the rapidly filling church, the men of the Coast Guard filed into the front rows.

"Paul!" Grandpa whispered loud enough for the whole congregation to hear. "There's Lieutenant Lipham. He's the one rescued you the day you snuck over to Assateague and your boat drifted away."

The lieutenant turned around, smiling broadly. Paul's cheeks reddened.

Maureen had secretly brought the birth announcements to church so that she and Paul could fill in the hour and date, everything except the name. But they never even opened the package. From almost the beginning of the sermon, they leaned forward, listening with every fiber.

"The earth is the Lord's," the deep voice of the preacher intoned. "He hath founded it upon the seas, and established it upon the floods."

And just by listening to the resounding voice, Paul and Maureen could see God commanding Noah to build the ark, big and flat-bottomed, and they could see the flood waters rising and the animals marching in, two by two.

"God is in the rescue business," the preacher's words

rolled out, "and every believer is a member of His rescue force. Today we pay special tribute to the United States Coast Guard. In the sight of God, men who do not know the harbor of His love are like men lost at sea, grasping for something or someone to save them. The Church is God's rescue force, just as the Coast Guard is the government's rescue force."

The preacher half-closed his eyes. "On Thursday night," he said, "when the last of the refugees staying here in our church had been taken to their homes or to the mainland, I walked down the streets and saw the havoc and the emptiness of our once lovely island. Yet no Chincoteaguer had lost his life, and I paused to thank God.

"Then I came back to the parsonage. All was dark and quiet. I was alone. Darkness was all around. Then a flash across the sky! The only light left shining came from the old lighthouse on Assateague Island. It was spreading wide its beam of hope and guidance. So it is when the lights of this old world are snuffed out, and the storms of life would destroy us, the steady light of God's love still shines. As our great Coast Guard keeps the light flashing from the lighthouse, so it is our task to keep our lights burning here at home.

"Let us sing."

Paul and Maureen were almost sorry when the sermon ended. They rose with the congregation, and sang as lustily as Grandma. Even Grandpa made his lips move as if he knew the words:

> "Brightly beams our Father's mercy
>   From His lighthouse evermore,
> But to us He gives the keeping
>   Of the lights along the shore."

Just as the final "Amen" faded, the preacher was handed a message. He read it to himself in apparent pleasure. Then he stilled the congregation.

"Friends," he said with a smile, "I have an important announcement." He cleared his throat and glanced at Paul and Maureen before he began. "On this day, in a stable in the city of Pocomoke, a foal was born—a tiny mare colt." He paused. Then he added, "And her mother is Misty."

There was a rustle as everyone turned to look at Paul and Maureen, then smiles and murmurs of "Misty . . . Misty" from every pew.

Quickly the congregation moved out into the bright sunshine. Preacher Britton was greeting the members, and Paul and Maureen, blushing in embarrassment, were standing beside him. Everyone was shaking hands with everyone else. Hands that all week had lifted and scrubbed and prayed now clasped each other in joy.

"It's the happiest news to reach Chincoteague in a week of terror!"

"The very happiest."

For once Grandpa didn't bolt for home as if his house were on fire. He shook hands heartily with the preacher. "Reverend," he said, "ye jes' put up one o' the greatest sermons I ever heerd!"

"Come oftener," the preacher replied with a grin.

Chapter 20

HOME AT LAST

AFTER RETURNING home from church, all of the Beebes hurried into old clothes and went to work in a kind of happy frenzy. Everything needed doing at once.

Paul crushed oats in Grandma's coffee grinder and mixed them with bran and linseed, all ready for the hot water when Misty came home. He filled the manger with good-smelling hay. He washed the salt block.

"Wouldn't surprise me none if ye licked it clean with yer own tongue," Grandpa laughed as he went by with Nanny's kid tugging at his pants leg.

In the kitchen Maureen was sewing strips of tape on an old blanket. Every now and then she ran to try it on Grandma to see if the ties were in the right place. "If it fits you, Grandma, it'll fit Misty."

172

Grandma made a wry face. "Reckon I should be complimented," she snorted, " 'stead of laying my ears back. Beats me!" she added as she wrapped jelly sandwiches in waxed paper. "There's barely a speck o' meal in the house for biscuits or bread, and scarce a dry thing to cover folks with, but there's allus oats and bran a-plenty, and a royal blanket for Miss Misty."

"Missus Misty!" Maureen corrected.

Grandma disappeared into her bedroom for a moment and came back with a shy smile. "Here's my contribution," she said. "Likely I'll have no more use for this soft baby blanket. With a couple of safety pins to fasten it under her belly, it'll be just the right size for Misty's young'un. That long ride home will be kind o' drafty for a newborn."

By half-past noon Grandpa and Paul and Maureen were waving good-bye to Grandma and were on their way to Pocomoke City. To their amazement, the causeway to the mainland was jammed with a long procession of cars coming from Maryland, Delaware, and even Washington, D.C.

"Why in tarnation they coming to Chincoteague today?" Paul asked, opening up the lunch box.

"I'll tune ye if I catch ye sayin' 'tarnation' again," Grandpa scolded. Then he cackled in laughter. " 'Tain't fittin' except fer an old feller like me."

"But why *are* they?" Maureen wanted to know.

"Folks is funny," Grandpa mused. "Some jes' nacherly likes to waller in woe like pigs in a pen. Sure as shootin' they're comin' to gawp at the wreckage and to take pitchers o' the boats in the streets, and the soggy beddin' and things dryin' in the sun. Curiosity folks, I calls 'em."

A station wagon with a Maryland license flagged them down. Brakes screeched for a mile as cars behind honked in a mad chorus. A young man with a shock of red hair called out, "How do we get to the Beebe Ranch? We want to see Misty's colt."

Grandpa stopped the truck and guffawed. "News out already?" he asked in amazement.

"Yes, sir! Network had it on the radio, and my kids gave me no peace—"

"Wal, what do ye know! Sorry, young feller, but you passed plumb by her. She's over to Pocomoke City, to Doc Finney's house." Grandpa drove on, chuckling.

"See!" Maureen said. "Not everybody comes to look at trouble."

"Ye're right, honey. Lucky thing yer Grandma stayed to home. She would've flew into the air, hearin' me talk like that."

When they reached Dr. Finney's place, the doctor, who had been watching from the house, came to meet them. With a welcoming smile he unlocked the gate and motioned Grandpa to drive in and park alongside the corral. Then without a word he led the way. In absolute silence the three Beebes walked one after the other Indian file behind him. They moved across the paddock as if it were hallowed ground. Still in silence they eased up to the barn. And then, after almost a year of waiting, the moment had come!

Unconsciously Grandpa took off his hat and tucked it under his arm. Paul and Maureen stood on tiptoe, peering in without breathing. They were utterly still, not wanting the scene to change. There, at the far end of the stall, stood

Misty. She eyed them dispassionately as if they belonged to another world and another time. Like a bird brooding a chick she was hovering over a wise little, fuzzy little, scraggly little foal. For a moment the tiny thing took fright and leaned quivering against her mother, who made soft whuffing sounds. Then, comforted, she nosed her way to Misty's teats and began nursing.

"Wa-al, I never!" Grandpa sighed in deep contentment. "Them sucky-smacky sounds is purtier 'n a hull flock o' meadow larks!"

Maureen brushed away a tear. How could a creature be so young and breakable-looking, and yet so spunky? "Why, I feel like I'm its grandma!" she whispered shyly. "And hasn't it got the longest eye-winkers and the curliest tail you most ever saw?"

Paul whispered too. "Look at the strange marking on her forehead—it's in the shape of a new sickle moon! I know!" he exulted. "That's 'cause she was born in the time of the new moon."

Grandpa stared. "She's the onliest colt I ever see with a markin' like that."

"Yes," Dr. Finney said. "There's nothing like her on the Eastern Shore."

"Likely not in all the world," Paul said.

After the colt had drunk her fill, Misty came to the door and nickered happily, sniffing Paul and Maureen by turns.

"She's inviting us in," Paul said.

Slowly, quietly, not to startle the little one, the Beebes went into the stall, and the gentlest of hands lifted her fore-lock that was only beginning to be a forelock. "Here's a girl's got a head on her," Grandpa approved. "There's enough Arabian into her to make that purty head. And ain't she marked up nice? Not a reg'lar map on her shoulders like her mommy, but she's got her four white stockings."

"And her color is sorrel, like Wings," Maureen said.

Dr. Finney looked at his watch, thinking of the calls still to be made.

Grandpa followed his glance. "If'n ye'll excuse us," he said, "we got to hyper along now. Any last-minute advice, Doc?"

"For now," Dr. Finney said, "avoid bulky food for Misty. Nothing rich or hard to digest."

"How about ground oats and bran and linseed?" Paul asked hopefully.

"Couldn't be better! And no need to remind you children that daily mucking-out is a MUST."

Grandpa nodded vigorously, an "I-told-you-so" twinkle in his eye.

"Right now their stall is the cleanest in the whole wide world," Maureen said proudly.

With quiet confidence she and Paul tied Misty's blanket in place for the trip back. Grandpa took the soft baby blanket and laid it on the little one. Then he crouched down and lifted her up in his arms and carried her out, with Paul leading Misty alongside.

As she approached the truck, Misty planted her feet and balked. Plain as day she bellered: "I'm *not* getting into that thing without my baby!" But when she found out that her foal was safely stowed in the cab in front, she hurried up the ramp, poked her head through the window, and nickered in relief.

Dr. Finney started to wave good-bye, then had a last-minute request. "Mind driving by David's window?" he asked. "I had to put him to bed this morning with a case of old-fashioned measles. Poor lad hasn't seen the colt. He's heartbroken."

Paul felt a prick of shame. "I'm sorry, Dr. Finney, I didn't even miss him." He reached into a pocket and pulled out a tiny wooden gull. "I made it to sell to the tourist folk," he explained, "but I want to give it to David instead. And some day," he added, warming to his own generosity, "I might make a carving of Misty and her foal. Just for him."

Grandpa drove home very carefully, avoiding ruts and bumps. He didn't want to jar the little filly, who lay asleep across Paul's and Maureen's laps, her soft woolen blanket rising and falling with her breathing.

Going over the causeway, they slowed to a crawl. One driver spotted Misty and put on the brakes so suddenly that his two children almost flew through the windshield. "There she is!" he shouted. "Hey, Mister, wait!"

Grandpa came to a stop, grinning. He felt good toward the whole world. "Want a picture?" he asked.

"Do we!" And now other cars were stopping and out popped dozens of children and dozens of cameras. Traffic stalled while shutters clicked on all sides.

After a few moments Misty began stomping and w
nying. There was a curious urging in her mind, a tremendou
pull for home.

"Let's go," Paul said. "Misty's getting nervous."

Grandpa stopped the picture-taking and drove on. And
at long last they were going down Beebe Road into Pony
Ranch. Once the tailgate was lowered Misty slow-footed
down the ramp like a queen returning to her kingdom.
Skipper, the official greeter, welcomed her in ten-foot bounds,

jumping, rolling, yelping in pure joy. And out on the marsh, Wings added his voice in a great cry of triumph.

Grandma rushed out of the house, calling, "Where's Misty's baby? Where?"

For answer Paul and Grandpa lifted her out of the truck and carefully set her down beside her mother. She tried a little caper, lost her balance and fell in a heap. Bravely she scrabbled up again, then staggered to her mother and began drinking thirstily. Satisfied, she blew bubbles, sending little beads of milk running down her whiskers.

Misty whickered in contentment. "Home at last," she seemed to say. And she gave the little rump at her side a nip, ever so gentle and motherly.

Chapter 21

A GRAVE DECISION

THAT NIGHT, when Pony Ranch had simmered down into a semblance of peace, Maureen brought out the birth announcements and piled them on the kitchen table. She and Paul were alone. Grandpa had gone to an emergency meeting of the Pony Penning Committee, and Grandma was attending the evening church service.

"You put the date on," Paul said to Maureen. "You write better than me. Besides, I got some important thinking to do."

"Oh?"

Paul flicked open his pocketknife and began working on a block of wood. Out of the corner of his eye he saw Maureen dip her pen in the ink bottle and wait with it poised in the air.

"I declare, Paul Beebe, you can be downright mean! What *are* you thinking?"

"And you can be such a *girl!*" Paul said in disdain. "Always poking and prying."

"All right, I won't ask. 'Cause I already know. So there!"

"What do you know?"

"You're trying to think of the right name for Misty's baby."

"Okay then. I reckon you got what Grandpa calls 'woman's tuition.' Now you know what's occupying my mind, whyn't you keep quiet and do your work?"

Sunday, March 11, 6 a.m. Maureen wrote again and again until her fingers were tired.

At last Paul was ready to talk. "There's three ways to do it. One is by her markings . . ."

"Like *New Moon* or *White Stockings,* Paul?"

"Uh-huh. And the second way is by using her family's names—like *Misty Wings* or *Pied Phantom.*"

"And what's the third way, Paul?"

Just then Grandpa's truck roared into the yard, brakes screeching. Grandpa himself banged into the house like a Fourth of July firecracker. He threw his hat on the peg, then with both hands began rubbing the bristles in his ears.

"I say there's *got* to be a Pony Pennin' this year like allus," he stormed. "Why, it's the oldest roundup in America! We jes' can't let folks down 'cause of a little flood. Why, come July and roundup time, folks are goin' to pack their night things and set out for Chincoteague hopin' to give their kids a real hollerday. And they're goin' to drive fer miles an' miles, and when they get here—NO hollerday! No

Pony Penning!" He snorted in disgust. "I won't hear to it! I jes'—"

"Grandpa!" Paul interrupted. "Who says there won't be a Pony Penning?"

"Why, the Mayor's committee and the firemen, they say ain't enough wild ponies left over to Assateague to make it excitin', and no money in the treasury to buy new ones.

"What's more," he bellowed, "they're right! But I ain't told 'em so! 'Cause without ponies this-here island is dead. Do ye think folks comes here to see oysters and clams and biddies?"

"No, Grandpa."

"Ye're dead right they don't! They come to see wild ponies swimmin' across the channel, and feudin' and fratchin' in the pens. Pony Penning Day! That's what they come fer. Can't see it nowhere else in the world."

Paul and Maureen were aghast. July without Pony Penning was unthinkable. "All year I been answering letters about Misty," Maureen said. "And in every one I invited people to come to Pony Penning, people from all over the United States. Even one to Alaska."

Paul broke in. "And this year folks'll come special on purpose to see Misty's baby."

Grandpa began pacing, thinking out loud. "If only we had the ponies! If only the Town Council could buy back some of the colts that was auctioned off last year and the year afore that."

He quickened his pace. "Why, we could load 'em onto a big old barge, and chug 'em acrost the channel to Assateague, and they'd go wild again jes' like they'd never left."

Now he spoke out with great conviction. "Why, then we could put up one o' the greatest Pony Pennings in Chincoteague history."

Grandpa ran out of breath. He gulped for more. "But all that'd take a heap o' money," he sighed.

"Maybe," Maureen said excitedly, "maybe Paul and me could earn a lot of money like we did to buy Misty's mother. We could rake clams or help people clean up their houses."

Paul looked pityingly at his sister. "When you going to grow up, Maureen? Why, it took us three whole months to earn enough to buy just one mare and her colt. Besides, folks here lost most everything in the flood. They can't afford to hire us."

"Paul's right, honey."

"But, Grandpa," Paul asked, "even if we had the money, would people sell back their ponies?"

"Likely some'd be right anxious to help," Grandpa replied, "and some'd sell fer other reasons. A lucky thing me and the Fire Company got a record o' each sale, and if only half them people say yes, that'd give us the start we need."

Grandpa suddenly remembered that his feet hurt. He collapsed into the nearest chair and began unlacing his Sunday shoes. "Can't abide 'em!" he grumbled. "I jes' stormed outen that meetin' afore it was done—half 'cause my hackles was up, but half 'cause my shoes squinched me."

The phone rang insistently. "You answer, Paul. There's another thing I can't abide. Phone-talkin'. A contraption o' the devil."

"It's for you, Grandpa. It's the Mayor and he sounds real important."

Grandpa thudded to the phone. "Hall–oo–oa!" he bellowed.

"Grandpa doesn't need a phone," Paul snickered. "He could just open a window."

"Sh!" Maureen put up a finger, listening.

"*Who* called you?" Grandpa questioned.

There was a pause.

"What in tunket *he* want?"

Another pause.

"He did!"

Paul and Maureen looked inquiringly at each other.

"Wa-al, Great Jumpin' Jehoshephat! Now ain't that nice? . . . What's that ye say?"

A long pause.

Still holding the receiver, Grandpa turned and looked penetratingly at Paul and Maureen. His voice sobered. "Sure I like the ideer, Mayor, but 'tain't fer me to say. I'll have to put it to Paul and Maureen and get their yes or no. The colt, nor Misty neither—they ain't mine, y'know."

Grandpa hung up the receiver and walked back to the table, collecting his thoughts. Paul and Maureen stared at him, unable to ask the question except with their eyes.

Grandpa hummed and hawed. "Now I ain't a-goin' to influence ye," he said. "It's *yer* druthers, an' no one else's."

"But what is it?"

"Y'see, uh, it's this way. One o' the big chiefs from the movie company that made Misty's picture—he jes' telephoned the Mayor long distance. From his home, mind ye."

"What did he want?" Maureen asked. "Does he want to make a picture of Misty's baby?"

"Stop interruptin'," Paul scolded. "Let Grandpa finish."

"Wa-al," Grandpa went on, "seems he'd been readin' 'bout the storm and how so many ponies had drowned. And he wants to do somethin' to help. Why, he's willin' to let theaters borry the picture of Misty free; that is, *if* the money tooken in goes to build up the lost herds."

Paul did a flying leap over his chair. "That's great, Grandpa. You don't have to get our okay on that."

"But I ain't told ye the kernel yet," Grandpa explained. "Y'see, the Mayor and the Council wants to start a disaster fund, and call it the Misty Disaster Fund." Grandpa stroked his chin and a far look crept into his eyes. "They want to cast Misty in the biggest role o' her life; even bigger'n bein' a star in a movie."

186

The children listened, speechless.

"Even bigger," Grandpa added, "than birthin' a colt."

"What could be bigger?" Maureen asked.

"They want Misty and her young'un to make a personal tour wherever her picture is playing, and go right spang up onto the stage. And part o' the ticket money'll be used to tidy up the island, but most of it to buy back the ponies. Mind ye, it'll all have to start right away. Mebbe in two weeks—that is, if there's to be a roundup this year."

Paul turned to his sister. "What do you say, Maureen?"

Maureen's face clouded and she thought carefully before replying. "If Misty's baby wasn't so new and tiny, I'd say yes."

Paul picked up the block of wood and his knife, and made a few fierce jabs. "Exactly the way I feel." He looked

at Maureen. " 'Course, it'd be fun to be excused from school and all."

"Mostly it'd be on Saturdays," Grandpa said drily.

"But suppose," Paul was serious now, "suppose they caught the shippin' fever, or bad coughs from travelin' and going in and out of hot theaters. Or even broke a leg."

All three of them lapsed into silence. No one knew what to say. Maureen screwed the cap onto the ink bottle as if she would never have need of it again. Paul threw his piece of wood into the stove and closed his knife. The silence was a growing power. Grandpa sat down and crossed his arms, using his paunch as a ledge. He looked up at the ceiling and across at the clock. He picked up one of the birth announcements and studied it. The corners of his mouth twisted into a smile of sympathy and understanding. "It'd be chancy," he admitted. "Mighty chancy."

"But suppose," Paul spoke slowly, earnestly, "suppose we let Misty and the colt go to just one theater, and if they come home feeling frisky, they could go again. But if they got sick or were off their feed for just one day, they'd *never* have to go again."

Grandpa's eyes shone like twin meteors. "Sometimes I think you two is the livin' image o' me! I'm so proud of ye I could strut like one o' our peacocks in full sail. I'll take it up with the Council first thing in the—"

Bong! Bong! . . . The clock struck the hour of ten, and with the last *bong* the telephone rang shrilly. Grandpa clapped a hand to his forehead, then grabbed for his shoes. "Great balls o' fire! I plumb forgot to pick up yer Grandma from the meetin' house. You answer, Maureen. I'm gone!"

Chapter 22

THE NAMING BEE

OVER THE WEEKEND the schoolhouse had been dried out, and on Monday it re-opened with only the high-tide mark showing. Paul and Maureen were present and on time. But it was a hard thing to remember the provinces of Canada, or to stand up and recite: "Washington, Adams, Jefferson, Madison, Monroe . . ." when Misty's filly had to be named. The Town Council was insistent. They had to have a name at once. And the more Paul and Maureen were pressed to make a decision, the harder it was to decide.

For the next few days, in school and out, they thought up names and just as quickly discarded them. None seemed right. Either they were too long, or when you called them out across the marsh they sounded puny. It wasn't like naming just any colt.

For three days they struggled. Then on Wednesday almost at dusk Mr. Conant, the postmaster himself, arrived at Pony Ranch with a whole bag of mail for the Beebes. When Grandma spied him striding across the yard, she quickly set an extra place at the table and sent Maureen to the door.

"Evenin', Mr. Conant," Maureen said politely, but her eyes were on the mailbag.

"How do you do, Maureen and Mrs. Beebe?"

"How-do, Mr. Conant. I declare," Grandma chuckled, "you look jes' like Santa Claus with that leather pouch ye're carryin'. Let me hang it on a peg whilst you set down. Mr. Beebe and Paul will be in right soon. Now then," she beamed, "do stay to supper. We got us a fine turtle stew with black-eyed peas, and light bread, and some of my beach-plum preserves."

"I'd be very honored to stay!" Mr. Conant replied. "My wife has taken her mother to Salisbury for over night, and while she has no doubt prepared some tasty treat for me, what is food without good talk to digest it?"

Grandma looked pleased. "That's what I allus tell Clarence, only I don't say it so elegant."

Maureen was still eyeing the mailbag, her curiosity at the bursting point.

"Oh, I almost forgot," Mr. Conant smiled broadly. He reached into his inside pocket and drew out an envelope bearing a bright red Special Delivery sticker. "It's for you and Paul," he said, handing it to Maureen. "Since it's marked *Special,* I decided to bring all of your mail along, instead of letting it wait until tomorrow." Pointing to the mailbag, he added, "It's the biggest batch of mail ever to come to Chincoteague for one family in one day."

There was a clatter and a stamping in the back hall as Grandpa and Paul came in. "Why, if 'tain't Mr. Conant,"

Grandpa said, putting out his hand. "I'm as pleased to see ye as a dog with two tails!"

"Look, Paul!" Maureen cried. "A letter, Special Delivery! For us!"

Paul took the news with outward calm, but his eyes strained to see the postmark and his fingers itched to snatch the letter and run off, like Skipper with a bone.

"You children put that letter with the others and wash up now," Grandma scolded gently as she stirred the stew. "Turtles is hard to come by, and I ain't minded to let our vittles get ruint. Besides," she said, "if it's good news, it'll keep, and if it's bad, time enough to read it after we've et. Everyone, please to sit. You here, Mr. Postmaster."

In spite of company, supper that night was, as Grandpa put it, "a lick and a gallop." Everyone was in a fever of excitement to start opening the letters. But first the table had to be cleared, and the crumbs swept clean. Then Grandma spread out a fresh checkered cloth to protect the top. "We allus use the kitchen table for everything," she explained to Mr. Conant, "fer readin' and writin', fer splintin' broken bird legs—whatever 'tis needs doin'." She nodded now in the direction of the mail pouch.

The postmaster took down the bag and dumped the letters onto the table. With the hand of an expert he stacked them in neat piles, placing the Special Delivery on top.

"It's like Christmas!" Maureen gasped.

"It's *bigger* than Christmas," Paul said.

"Who they for?" Grandpa wanted to know.

"Some are for you, Mr. Beebe, and some for Paul and Maureen."

Wait-a-Minute jumped on the table and began upsetting the piles. Paul swept her off with his arm. "You tend to your kittens," he said not unkindly. "We got important business!" He took out his pocketknife. "I'll do the slitting," he announced.

"I'll do the pullin' out and unfoldin'," Grandpa offered.

"You read them to us, Grandma," Maureen said. "You make everything sound like a storybook."

Grandma blushed. "Mr. Conant's got the edification. I'd be right shy readin' in front of him."

"Not at all, not at all, Mrs. Beebe. I agree with Maureen. Many a Sunday I've gone by your class and heard you reading from the Bible. I feel complimented you let me stay and be part of the family."

For a moment the slitting of the envelopes and the crackle of paper were the only sounds in the room. Then Grandma picked up the Special Delivery letter, took a deep breath, and in her best Sunday voice began:

"Dear Paul and Maureen,
I am sorry the storm came. But I am glad Misty had a baby. Was I surprised!
I hope some day I can visit your island or maybe even live there. I hope to go to Pony Penning Day and maybe buy a pony.
I hope you don't mind if I send you a name for Misty's baby. I think 'Windy' would be nice."

"By ginger!" Grandpa exclaimed. "That's uncommon purty. Let's have another, Idy."

Mr. Conant took pencil and paper out of his pocket and wrote down *Windy* with a checkmark after it.

"This one is to Misty herself," Grandma went on. "Why, it's a regular baby card, and it says, *Congratulations to you and the new little bundle of joy."*

"Turn it over, Grandma, there's a note on the back," Maureen said.

"So there is! Listen:

"Dear little Misty,
I've heard so much about you I feel like I know you. I love horses and I was worried about you

194

during the storm. You have a wonderful master and mistress to bring you into the kitchen.

You should name your filly 'Misty's Little Storm Cloud.'

Isn't that beautiful, folks?"

Grandpa looked inquiringly at the children. "To my notion," he hesitated, "it'd be too long a handle fer such a little mite—even if we was to boil it down some."

Maureen was impatient. "More, Grandma. More!"

"Here's one from a fifth-grader up to Glassboro, New Jersey:

"I am a boy ten and a half years old. This is not a very long letter, but I like the name 'Windy' for Misty's colt."

Mr. Conant made a second checkmark after *Windy*. "Two for *Windy*," he announced.

"Doggone, if this ain't jes' like an election," Grandpa said. "Vote countin' and all."

Grandma broke out in smiles. "This one's mostly questions:

"Dear Paul and Maureen,

How are you? I am fine. I read in the paper that Misty is safe.

How do you pronounce your island's name?

If I should come to your island, would you show me how to eat oysters?

How are your Grandpa and Grandma? I think you are one of the greatest families in the U.S.A.

P.S. Do you think you'll have a Pony Penning this year?"

"See?" Maureen said. "Folks are asking already, but I just won't answer this one until later. Go on, Grandma."

"Here's one from a lady teacher:

"We read in the paper that Misty had a filly and also that 145 ponies died. My heart just sinks.

One of my pupils said that colts have such twinkly legs he thought 'Sand Piper' would be a good name for Misty's baby."

"Hmmm," Paul said approvingly. "See what I mean, Maureen? *Sand Piper* would honor her granddaddy, the Pied Piper."

Mr. Conant wrote down the name with one checkmark and a star beside it.

"If she was a horse-colt instead of a mare-colt," Maureen said, "I'd like it fine. But we got to think about when she's grown up."

Mr. Conant erased the star.

Grandma pursed her lips as she read the next letter to herself.

"Land sakes, Idy, I'll be a bushy-whiskered old man by the time ye make that one out."

"Oh, it's easy to make out," she replied. "The writing's beautiful. It's to you, Clarence." She held it up for all to see. Then she cleared her throat:

"Dear Sir:

I cut a picture from the state paper yesterday of Misty's filly, born Sunday, March 11th. The caption said she was foaled at an animal hospital, but I am hoping that someone in your town can give me more information about her. Is she healthy? And is she for sale?"

There was a stunned silence. Grandpa's face went red and the cords of his neck bulged.

Mr. Conant looked at him in alarm. "Mr. Beebe," he said, "I know the answer to that one. If you'll allow me, I'd like to do the replying."

Grandpa didn't trust himself to speak. He managed a nod of thanks.

"Grandma, try another!" Maureen urged.

"Here's a real short one," Grandma said cheerily, "and it says:

"If I owned Misty, I would name her colt 'Stormy.'"

Paul's eyes met Maureen's and held. Then he leaped up from his chair, stood on his head, and cried, "Ya-hoo!" In an instant he was right side up again. He shouted the name, "STORMY!" Then he whispered it very softly, *"Stormy."*

Maureen clapped her hands. "Why, it sounds good both ways!"

Promptly Mr. Conant wrote it down. "I'll give this one two stars," he said.

And still there were more letters and more names— *Gale Winds* and *Rip Tide* and *Sea Wings* and *Ocean Mist* and *Misty's Shadow* and *Mini Mist* and *Foggy* and *Cloudy* —until at last they were down to one letter.

Grandpa loosened his suspenders, yawning and stretching. "Out with that last one, Idy. Sandman's workin' on me, both barrels."

Grandma's face lighted with pleasure. "Why, it's signed by a whole bunch of school children over to Reistertown, Maryland." She adjusted her spectacles and began:

"Our class read the book about Misty. Now we are reading about the awful storm that flooded your island. We are glad Misty was not drowned. As soon as we heard the news about her colt, we decided to write you. We think you should name her 'Stormy' because she was born in a storm. Would you like that? We would. We had a secret ballot, and 'Stormy' won first place with twenty votes."

Paul drew in his breath. "That does it!" he said. "Remember, Maureen? Sometimes they name 'em for markings, sometimes for ancestors, and the third way is for natural phenom . . . happenings of Nature."

"Like the storm?"

"Exactly." Paul got up from the table and spoke now in great seriousness. "Mr. Conant, how many votes do we have for *Stormy?*"

"Twenty-two, Paul."

"All those in favor of *Stormy* please say Aye."

The Ayes were loud and clear.

Maureen heaved a great sigh. "Oh, Paul, now we can fill in the announcements."

Chapter 23

DRESS REHEARSAL

IT WAS unanimous! The Town Council, the Firemen, the Ladies' Auxiliary, Preacher Britton, and of course the Postmaster—everyone approved the name *Stormy*. Stormy, they said, was the one good thing to come out of the storm.

News of the Misty Disaster Fund swept the Eastern Shore. Theater owners all up and down the coast wanted to present the famous ponies on their mission of mercy.

Now that Paul and Maureen had agreed to a tryout, they entered into the project with enthusiasm. "It's got to be good!" Paul kept repeating. "If children are going to spend their allowance money, they're entitled to a real show."

"Why, Paul, the movie of Misty is a beautiful show," Maureen said in a hurt tone.

"Sure it is. But lots of folks have seen it. What they want now is to see Misty herself and little Stormy. Even the Mayor says so."

The performance in the big city of Richmond was scheduled for a week from Saturday. That left only ten days to do a million things, big and little.

They scrubbed Misty's stepstool and gave it a fresh coat of paint, bright blue. And the moment it was dry, and a dozen times each day, they made her step up on it and shake hands vigorously, just for practice. Often while she shook hands, Stormy nursed her.

"Makes Misty seem ambi-dextrous," Paul said.

Grandpa chortled. "Reckon you could call it that. I swan, the way that gal shakes hands on the slightest excuse it looks like she's campaignin'."

"She is!" Maureen said. "She's campaigning for the Misty Disaster Fund."

"Maureen, you go get my nippers," Grandpa ordered. "I better trim them hoofs. She's shakin' hands so high she's liable to plant her hoofograph on some little younker's head."

As for Stormy, working on her was pure joy. Every night after school Paul and Maureen curried and combed her, not to make her less fuzzy, but to get her used to something besides Misty's tongue. And gradually they halter-broke her. Of course, there wasn't a halter anywhere on the island—or even in Horntown or Pocomoke—tiny enough to fit. Paul had to make one out of wickie rope, just as he had done for Misty when she was a baby. And after a little urging Grandma gave up her favorite piece of chest flannel to wrap around the noseband of the halter.

200

"Just feel of it now, Grandma," Paul exclaimed. "It's as soft as the lamb's wool they use for racehorse colts."

"Don't need to feel it. I know," Grandma said drily.

Stormy accepted the halter with only a little head tossing. Occasionally as she was being led about, she turned to gaze at Skipper and the kid as much as to say: "Hey, you! Why can you two run free?"

For answer they blatted and barked and dared her to join in the fun. But Misty wouldn't let her. When they came too close, she leaped at them, lashing out with her forefeet, head low, teeth bared. They quickly got the message, scattered in panic, and stayed away for hours.

As Saturday approached, everything was ready except the old truck. How ugly and drab it seemed for a movie star and her filly! It needed paint and polish and a new floor and a new top. But there was no money and no time to do anything about it.

Then late on Friday, just before darkness closed in, Mr. Hancock arrived looking pleased as a boy. He took a long bundle from his car and with a proud flourish unrolled two enormous pieces of canvas. On each he had painted a life-size picture of Misty and Stormy. "To cover the sides of your truck," he said proudly. "I want the folks in Richmond to know that us Chincoteaguers do things up right."

Now even the truck was resplendent and gay!

By six o'clock the next morning, chores were done and Grandpa and the children were loading up the truck. Grandma and Skipper, Nanny and the kid were clustered about, watching, as Misty walked up the ramp in eager anticipation. She could smell the sweet hay aboard and the juicy slices of a Delicious apple tucked here and there. Little Stormy skittered along after her, with Paul and Maureen on either side, arms spread-eagled to keep her from falling off.

"I feel so left-behind," Grandma said, folding and unfolding her hands in her apron. "Like a . . . well, like a colt that's bein' weaned."

Grandpa was about to break into laughter, but when he saw Grandma's woebegone face, he came over to her, his voice full of tenderness. "Tide o' life's flowin' normal again, eh, Idy? The goin' out and the comin' in."

"Sure, Grandma," Maureen said, "and we'll be home afore dark."

"And hungry as bears," added Paul.

Grandma blinked hard. "I reckon the storm's brought us so close I hate to lose sight o' ye, even for a day." Big tears began running down her face.

"Idy!" Grandpa bellowed. "You come with us. Call up them Auxiliary ladies and tell 'em you can't sew on the children's band uniforms today. What if the old ones did float out to sea? Tell the kids to play in their birthday suits! Tell 'em anything. Tell 'em we can't load and unload the ponies without your help."

Suddenly the tension was gone. Grandma wiped her tears with a corner of her apron and began laughing at the thought of her lifting the ponies. "Now be off with you. I can't stand out here all day. I got a pile of work to do."

But as the truck swung out of the drive, she didn't go into the house. Her eyes followed it to the road, as she continued wrapping and unwrapping her arms in her apron. Then suddenly she took off the apron and waved good-bye.

Paul turned and waved back. He could see Grandma growing smaller and farther away, standing in front of the sign that said "Misty's Meadow." And even while he was feeling sorry for her, having to do up the dishes and go to the Ladies' Auxiliary and all, his mind raced ahead to Richmond. In sudden panic he wondered, Would there be anyone at the theater at all? Maybe the day was too nice, and children would be shooting marbles and flying kites and playing baseball, and they had seen the movie anyway.

Chapter 24

STORMY'S DEBUT

IN RICHMOND, a hundred and twenty miles away, children of all ages were waking up, springing out of bed, aware that this morning held a delicious sense of adventure and wonder. They dressed more quickly than usual and fretted at grown-ups who dilly-dallied over breakfast. They wanted to be sure of getting to the theater on time.

A few of the children could boast of having seen real actors making personal appearances, and some had even seen animal actors like Trigger and Lassie. But no one ever had seen the live heroes of a story that had really and truly happened. It was almost too exciting to think about.

The employees of the Byrd Theater, too, felt an enthusiasm they could not define. By nine o'clock the manager arrived, just out of the barber chair. He was followed closely by the projectionist, who disappeared into his cubicle under the ceiling. Then came the cashier, the popcorn-maker, and the ticket-taker, followed by the musicians with their cellos and piccolos and kettledrums.

And last of all, the ushers and the doorman in bright blue uniforms with gold braid and buttons.

By ten minutes after nine all was in readiness: the lights blazing, the film threaded properly, the orchestra tuning up, popcorn popping and filling the lobby with its tantalizing smell; and, most important, a special ramp was snubbed up tight against the stage. To test it, the manager stomped up the ramp and stomped back down again as if he were a whole cavalcade of horses. "Solid as the Brooklyn Bridge!" he said in satisfaction.

By nine-fifteen the ushers took their posts, the doorman opened the plate-glass doors, and down in the pit the orchestra began playing "Pony Boy, Pony Boy, won't you be my Pony Boy?" At the same time the pretty cashier climbed to her perch in her glass cage.

By nine-sixteen she was looking out the porthole saying, "How many, please?" "Thank you." "How many, please?" "Thank you." Her fingers flew to make change and tear off the right number of tickets.

No one, not even the manager, was prepared for the swarms of people coming all at once—Boy Scouts and Cub Scouts, Girl Scouts and Brownies, Campfire Girls and Bluebirds, classes from schools, from churches, from orphanages, families of eight and ten, with neighbor children in tow. It was a human river, so noisy with shuffling and shouting that even the drums in the orchestra could scarcely be heard.

By nine-forty every seat on the first floor was taken. By nine-fifty the balcony was filling up, and by one minute to ten there was not a seat left anywhere, not even in the second balcony. From floor to ceiling the theater was packed.

At the stroke of ten the asbestos curtain went up, the ponderous red velvet curtains parted, and the house lights dimmed, except for the tiny red bulbs at the exits. With a crash of cymbals the music stopped. A hush spread over the theater and rose like heat waves from a midsummer hayfield.

Then in all that breathless quiet the picture flashed on the screen, and suddenly Time ceased to exist. A thousand people were no longer in a darkened theater. They were transported to a wind-rumpled island with sea birds crying and wild ponies spinning along the beach. By pure magic

they were playing every role. They were roundup men spooking out the wild ponies from bush and briar, and suddenly coming upon the Phantom with her newborn foal, Misty. And then they *were* that foal, struggling to swim across the channel, struggling to keep from being sucked down into a whirlpool. And in a flash they were a daring tow-headed boy, jumping into the sea, grabbing Misty's forelock, pulling her to safety.

Even the ushers in the aisle were caught up in the spell —cheering when the Phantom raced Black Comet and won; laughing when Misty came flying out of Grandma's kitchen; gulping their tears when Paul bade farewell to the beautiful wild mare who was Misty's mother.

An unmistakable sniffling filled the theater as THE END

207

flashed upon the screen. Grownups and children smiled at each other through their tears as if they had come through a heartwarming experience together.

Then a handful of boys in the balcony began shouting: *"We want Misty. We want Stormy!"* And the whole audience took up the chant.

From the wings the manager walked briskly onto the stage. His face was one wide happy smile. He raised his hand for silence. "Boys and girls!" he spoke into the microphone. "Thank you for coming to this gala performance. All of the proceeds today—every penny you paid—will be used to restore the island of Chincoteague and to rebuild the herds of wild ponies on Assateague."

The applause broke before he had finished. He opened his lips to say more, but the same handful of boys shouted, *"We want Misty. We want Stormy."* And again the whole audience joined in. *"We want Misty. We want Stormy!"*

When the chant showed no signs of diminishing, the manager shrugged helplessly, then signaled to the stagehand. As if he had waved a wand, the lights went out, one by one, until the theater was in total blackness. An utter quiet fell as a slender beam of light played up and down the left aisle. It steadied at a point underneath the balcony.

And there, from out of the darkness into the shaft of light stepped two ponies. They were led by a spry-legged old man and flanked by a boy and a girl, but no one saw them for they were lost in shadow. Every eye was riveted on the two creatures tittupping down the aisle—one so sure-footed and motherly, one so little and wobbly.

From a thousand throats came the whispered cry,

"There they are!" And the murmuring grew in power like water from a dike giving way. The children in the balconies almost fell over the railing in their urgency to see. And down below, those on the aisle reached out with their arms, and those not on the aisle crowded on top like a football pile-up, and the fingers of all those hands stretched out to feel the furry bodies.

The theater manager cried out in alarm: "Don't touch the ponies—you might be kicked!" But it was like crying to the sun to stop shining or the wind to stop blowing.

With his body Paul tried to protect Stormy and Misty. But they didn't want protection. They were enjoying every minute of their march down the aisle.

And now the little procession has reached the ramp to the stage. Misty walks up calmly, in almost human dignity, and with only a little pushing from behind, Stormy joins her. The stage is ablaze with light so that the audience is nothing but a black blur, far away and quiet now. Misty looks around her at the big bright emptiness. It is bigger than her stall at home, bigger even than Dr. Finney's stable. Her eyes give only a passing glance to the artificial palm trees. Then they pounce on the one thing she recognizes. Her stepstool! In seeming delight she goes over and steps up with her fore-feet, nickering to Stormy: "Come to me, little one."

Stormy shows a moment of panic. Her nostrils flutter in a petulant whinny. Then, light as thistledown, she skitters across the stage. And with all those faces watching, she nuzzles up to her mother and begins nursing, her little broomtail flapping in greedy excitement.

So deep a silence hangs over the theater that the sounds of her suckling go out over the loud speakers and carry up to the second balcony. In quiet ecstasy each child is hugging Stormy to himself in wonder and love.

Done with her nursing the filly turns her head, wiping her baby whiskers on Paul's pants leg. The audience bursts into joyous laughter.

The spell is broken. Misty jostles her foal and nips along her neck just in fun; then she licks her vehemently as if to make up for that long separation during the ride from Chincoteague.

All this while none of the human creatures on the stage had spoken a word. But suddenly Grandpa was over his stage fright. "If Misty ain't careful," he bellowed to the last row in the balcony, "she'll erase them purty patches off'n Stormy."

The children shrieked. When at last they had quieted down, Grandpa thanked them in behalf of all the people of Chincoteague, and the ponies that were left, and the new ones which their money was going to buy.

"And Stormy thanks you, too." Grandpa set her up on the stepstool alongside her mother, and they posed with their heads close together even when a flash bulb popped right in their faces.

Then Grandpa selected one boy from the audience and one girl and invited them up on the stage so that Misty could shake their hands and so thank everyone. Eagerly the two children ran up the ramp, but once on the stage they suddenly froze, their arms rigid at their sides. It was Misty who without any prompting offered her forefoot first. Then timid hands reached out, one at a time, to return the gesture. But again it was Misty who did the pumping and enjoyed the whole procedure.

Grandpa threw back his head and howled. Still chuckling he explained, "In my boy-days I was an organ-pumper on Sundays. If only I'd of had a smart pony like Misty, she could've done it fer me!"

Then a man went up the aisles with a microphone, and children asked their questions right into it.

"Was Misty really in your kitchen during the storm?"

"Was it funny to see a pony looking out your kitchen window, instead of Grandma?"

"Why are colts mostly legs?"

"How many days old is Stormy?"

"How many ponies will the firemen buy with our money?"

"Will they go wild again on Assateague?"

"Did Grandma get mad at Misty messing in the house?"

"Did Wings live through the storm?"

Grandpa patiently answered each question, with a nod and smile of agreement from Paul and Maureen. With dozens of eager hands still waving for attention, time ran out. The musicians started playing "America, the Beautiful," while Misty and Stormy went down the ramp and up the other aisle this time so that more hands could reach out and touch.

The sun seemed brighter than ever when the little procession reached the door of the theater. Paul and Maureen drew a deep breath. It had been a rousing, heart-lifting performance, and they knew they had never been so happy.

Chapter 25

THE LAST SCENE

IT WAS afternoon before Misty and Stormy were loaded
into the truck for the long drive home. All the way Grandpa
and the children sat in quiet contentment, too full for words.
They rode in silence, each one tasting his own memories of
the performance, each one filled to the brim with a deep,
almost spiritual happiness.

The pine trees were throwing long shadows and the sun
was slipping into Chincoteague Bay when they arrived back
at Pony Ranch. Grandma came hurrying out to meet them,
her eyes asking a dozen questions. She waited expectantly for
the news, but all she got was a "Hi, Grandma. It was great!"

Grandma buttoned her sweater against the evening breeze and sat down to watch the unloading. "No use pressin' now; else I'll only get half the story," she told herself. "Allus the ponies come first. I'll bide my time." Nanny shouldered up to her, butting very gently. Unconsciously Grandma tucked her skirt out of Nanny's reach. Then she settled herself to watch and wait.

Grandpa and the children were like actors working in pantomime. Each one knew exactly what to do. Paul lowered the tailgate of the truck and led Misty down to the fence. Grandpa picked up Stormy, carried her out and set her beside Misty. Maureen took off Stormy's halter. Then she and Paul quickly went around to the gate to let the bars down. But before even the top one was lowered, Misty did something she had done only as a yearling. From a standing start she leaped nimbly over the bars and landed inside. Then she turned around as if wondering what to do about her youngster. Stormy let out a frightened squeal, then with head and tail low, she scrambled under the bars and found her mother.

The twilit quiet ended in a crash of noise. A gaggle of geese rose in a honking cloud, the peacock let out a hair-chilling scream, Skipper yelped, the goats blatted. Even Grandpa swelled the racket. "By thunder!" he boomed. " 'Twas quieter in that there movie house with a thousand kids screeching."

In the midst of all the confusion Misty let Stormy nurse, but only for a matter of seconds. After the long hours of being a sedate mother, she suddenly had to be a wild pony again. She took off down the pasture in a quick streaking run, Stormy hopping along behind.

Look at that little tyke go!" Paul exclaimed.

Maureen cried out in sudden alarm as Misty began crow-hopping, twisting, swerving, kicking at the sky. "Stormy'll get hurt!" she screamed.

But Stormy was trying out little kicks of her own, kiting away, falling to her knees, picking herself up, yet always keeping out of reach.

"She knows just how far to stay away," Paul laughed proudly.

"Why, they're brimful of spirit after all the doin's!" Grandma exclaimed. "Wisht I felt like that."

"*I* feel spry as a hopper-grass," Grandpa boasted.

"So do I," Maureen said.

"I don't," Paul declared. "I feel better . . . and bigger . . . and wilder."

"How do you mean, Paul?" Grandma asked.

He pointed a finger to the darkening sky. "See that gull 'way up yonder heading into a cloud?"

"Uh-hmm."

"Well, I can fly up there right alongside him."

Grandma took off her spectacles to study the white soaring wings tipped with the last gold of the sun. "You can?" She smiled at him in pleased wonder. "Even without wings?"

Paul nodded, embarrassed, not knowing how to explain.

There was a strained silence. At last he spoke in a hushed voice, "Grandma, today in the theater I felt and knew things I never knew before."

Grandpa put an arm around Paul and another around Maureen. "I know jes' what he means, Idy. And I don't think no one—not their teacher, nor the postmaster, and mebbe not even Preacher Britton—could really put it to words. Idy, to those city kids in Richmond, today was like a fairy story come to life. It meant something real to 'em. And you'd of thought Misty and Stormy was borned actors, the way they played their parts." He sighed in deep satisfaction. "Fer oncet everything come out jes' 'zackly perfect. And fer oncet in my lifetime I'm too happy to eat."

Misty and Stormy seemed to feel the same way. Their kicking and cavorting done, they turned tail on their friends and walked down the meadowland toward their pine grove by the sea.

It was like the end of a play, their walking off, slow-footed and contented, side by side. Without benefit of words they were playing the last scene. It was good to be out under the big sky. And good to breathe in the fresh, clean air. And how cool the marshy turf felt to their feet. Home was a good place to be.

Epilogue

TO MAKE THE STORY COMPLETE

Misty and little Stormy showed no ill effects, even the next day, because of their trip to the theater. They were, as Grandpa Beebe said, "borned actors." They seemed to burst into bloom like the daffodils after the storm. And so they traveled to more and more theaters. Each time they seemed eager to go, eager to meet their enraptured audiences, and deliriously happy to come back home.

At the end of the tour there was money enough to start the Volunteer Firemen buying back the ponies sold in other years.

But this is only half the story. While Misty and Stormy were doing their part, boys and girls all over the United States were helping, too. They deluged Chincoteague with a fresh tide—of letters! From big cities and tiny hamlets they came, and tucked inside were pennies, dimes, and dollars.

The letters are stories in themselves:

Here is a check for four dollars and four cents for the Misty Disaster Fund. It is an odd number because we earned it weeding dandelions and they grow odd. We hope the money will come in handy. Please excuse our poor writing. We are doing this in my tree house.

We had a lemonade stand and Mother didn't charge us for the lemons. We made three dollars to help restore your herds. We think the new ponies will be glad to go wild again.

I was sad to hear of your disasterous flood because I feel like Misty and Phantom and the Pied Piper are my friends. I know that a quarter is just a drop in the bucket, but I hope that enough people send in "drops" to fill it up.

The radio said your ponies and chickens drowned. I will send you a surprise with this letter. It is one dollar. I know that isn't much, but that's how much I can give.

We all voted to give our class treasury of five dollars to the Misty Disaster Fund so you can buy a whole pony in the name of us fifth graders. We want Pony Penning Day to go on forever.

I been picking blueberries all day and here's my fifty cents. Give my regards to Misty.

During our Story Hour we set out a jar marked "For Pony Pennies," and we marched around the library until 386 pennies were dropped in.

We are a group of 4-H girls, 10 to 16 years old. Every year we have a horse show and we do all the planning, fixing rings, making jumps, and getting prizes and ribbons. From our proceeds this year we want to give a hundred dollars to help replenish the herds that were drowned.

Day by day the Misty Disaster Fund grew and grew. By June the firemen had bought back enough ponies to restore the herds on Assateague. And on the last Wednesday of July the annual roundup and Pony Penning took place just as it has for over a hundred years.

222

Thousands of visitors came, and they marveled at how quickly the new ponies had gone back to their wild ways. The celebration was a rousing success.

Of course Stormy and Misty were on hand where everyone could see and pet them. *They* were not wild at all. Yet they were the heroes of the day.

For their help the author is grateful to

RALPH AND JEANETTE BEEBE, uncle and aunt
of Paul and Maureen

SAM BENDHEIM, SR., AND SAM BENDHEIM, JR.,
President and Vice President of the
Byrd Theaters, Richmond, Va.

THE REVEREND RAYMOND BRITTON, Chincoteague

WARREN CONANT, Postmaster of Chincoteague,
and his wife, PAULINE

DR. GARLAND E. FINNEY, JR., veterinarian
of Pocomoke, Md., and his wife, MARAH

MILES HANCOCK, terrapin trapper and wood-
carver, Chincoteague

LT. WILLIAM LIPHAM, U.S. Coast Guard

WILLIAM E. NICHOLS, JR., Councilman of
Chincoteague

ROBERT N. REED, Mayor of Chincoteague

TOM REED, naturalist, Chincoteague

JOYCE TARR, map maker, Chincoteague

224